Rapture the Chronicles
Judgment Day

D1641968

Richard D. VanderPloeg

The Rapture Chronicles Judgment Day™

The Rapture Chronicles: Judgment Day, is the 4th book in a series that collectively contains over 10,000 hours of the author's research along with his commentaries and higher guidance.

Scriptures taken from the New King James Version®. Copyright © 1982 by Thomas Nelson, Inc. Used by permission. All rights reserved.

This work is classified by the author as, Opinion Based Realistic Fiction. Opinion Based Realistic Fiction typically involves a story whose basic setting (time and location in the world) is real and whose events could feasibly happen in that real-world setting. Ref: Wikipedia, the free encyclopedia.

With respect to any resemblance to locales, organizations, or persons is entirely coincidental and fictional and beyond the intent of either the author or the publisher.

Contact Information: www.theRaptureChronicles.com
Cover background picture, used with permission.
Getty Images File Number: 2055067222

QUAD SERIES WITH PREQUEL
Book One, the Rapture Chronicles: AFTERMATH
ISBN: 978-0-9867562-5-2
Book Two, the Rapture Chronicles: MARSHALL LAW
ISBN: 978-0-986-7562-6-9
Book Three, the Rapture Chronicles: ZOMBIES
ISBN: 978-0-9867562-7-6
Book Four, the Rapture Chronicles: JUDGMENT DAY
ISBN: 978-0-9867562-8-3
Prequel, the Rapture Chronicles: EXODUS PROTOCOL
ISBN: 978-0-9867562-9-0
Printed in the United States of America.

DEDICATION

Praise **God**.

"For many are called, but few are chosen."

"By now you know who spoke these words and to whom"

Now, we see how the 'bad & good' live during the next 1000-years.

Evil, Terminating into Oblivion 'as the sand of the sea'

… 'Life Eternal for the saved.'"

SYNOPSIS

"Book-4, begins with Tom, Maria and Joe being escorted out of the King's Marriage Feast Hall by "You know who" and into the time known as the 1000-year Kingdom... "Peace for some, no peace for most!"

The Redeemed, now in their Heavenly bodies dwell within the New Jerusalem, having at its center God's Holy mountain many hundreds of miles high.

The New Jerusalem is about 1400 miles square and has four mighty walls with a total of twelve gates of pearl, four on each of its sides, and is tethered to Heaven above it.

Israelites, from Adam onwards who have been called back to life by God, save and except those who participated in the "Cull of the Damned during Armageddon" live outside, encompassing the New Jerusalem, in twelve tribes.

They are given the opportunity to live a God-fearing-life for 1000-years and in doing so their names are erased from the Judgment Day Books and entered into the Book of Life. They are still in their mortal bodies and no one will die from natural causes during these days.

They are taught by God's Royal Kings, Royal Priests and Priests of various distinctions.

The <u>bad</u> and the <u>good</u> from the King's Marriage Feast Hall, surround the 12 tribes of Israel, who themselves encompass the New Jerusalem, in concentric circles.

The bad, soon begin migrating to the outer regions of the now-rejoined land masses and Satan's evil-seeds now germinate into the anti-God.

Evil is alive and well, and soon Gog is seen in the northern half and his Magog commanders and nations, in the southern half. In time, these anti-God numbers multiply into the Biblical... "Sand of the Sea."

Evil is kept in check from hurting all who are living in peace outside the walls of the New Jerusalem in the 12 Tribes, and also those who live in peace, surrounding them, by God's Royal Kings and Royal Priests.

They have been given immensely powerful energy weapons, biblically described as 'rods of iron'.

The full scope of these energy-weapons will amaze and comfort the 'good' and 'panic' the bad to flee from their presence.

Towards the end of the 1000-years Satan is set loose from his confinement pit for 15 months.

Also released at this time are his 3-demons, as described in the book of Daniel 7:11-12

"I watched then because of the sound of the pompous words which the horn was speaking; I watched till the beast was slain, and its body destroyed and given to the burning flame.

As for the rest of the beasts, they had their dominion taken away, **yet their lives were prolonged for a SEASON AND A TIME."**
(15 months)

Satan, and his 3 remaining demons (Daniel's vision) are released for 15 months and are roaming among billions of evil seeds, masquerading as humans. The leader of these billions of anti-God is a demonically possessed human being named Gog; along with him are his Magog commanders. Even though these demons are supernatural, and their abilities have been taken away, they are extremely effective at riling up the anti-God for (unbeknownst to them) their last battle.

Evil, now advances towards God's New Jerusalem including the Israelites and those deemed worthy and good by God, living in peace.

Evil, prepares for war, and amasses billions of Satan's evil seeds whose numbers by now are recorded as 'the sand of the sea,' the anti-God races.

Evil, commences its final attack… they chose poorly.

Evil, is consumed by God's Fire, its flesh is incinerated, but not its bones, which have a future-purpose.

Judgment Day

The Judgment Days Books are now open… if your name is still recorded in them,

the second death then applies, and your body-soul-spirit goes into oblivion.

Book of Life

Those who during the 1000-years, who have proven themselves worthy to God, have by now had their names erased from the Judgment Day Books and entered into the Book of Life."

They form the eternal citizens of the…
New Heaven and New Earth.

Lamb's Book of Life

This is a most glorious book…those in this book are *absolutely divine*!

7 YEAR GREAT TRIBULATION

The TWO WITNESSES of GOD who testify to the entire world begin at day-1040 T/d. This is 220-days still within the first half of the 7 years. This allows for their work to be completed in 2300 days and not 2520 days.

2300 Days "until the Sanctuary is Cleansed"

TIME OF REFINEMENT
1260 DAYS

REFINED
CHILDREN OF GOD
MARTYRS OF UNDERSTANDING
CHRISTIAN MARTYRS OF CHRIST

- WAR IN HEAVEN
- DRAGON HURLED TO EARTH
- WOMAN FLEES
- WILDERNESS SANCTUARY
- DRAGON'S HUGE SERGE FLOOD WAVES
- GREAT DOMED CITY
- RISE OF THE "UNHOLY TRINITY"
- DRAGON'S TATTOO 666, 3-COLOR
- CHRISTIANS PERSECUTED
- FLEE TO THE HILLS
- ROCKY MOUNTAIN SANCTUARY

1040 T/D
- TWO WITNESSES   BEGIN
- ZOMBIE PLAGUES   BEGIN
- HELL MONSTERS   BEGIN

1260 T/D
- POWER OF THE HOLY PEOPLE SHATTERED
- GOD'S WILDERNESS CHILDREN "REFINED"
- MARTYRS OF UNDERSTANDING "REFINED"
- DRAGON BREAKS PEACE TREATY

1290 T/D
- DRAGON'S IMAGE-IDOL COMPLETED
- DRAGON'S TEMPLE DEDICATION CEREMONY
- ABOMINATION OF DESOLATION ACTIVATED
- DRAGON'S IMAGE IDOLS WORLDWIDE
- DRAGON'S TATTOO 666, 1-COLOR, GET ITS MARK ON RIGHT HAND, OR DIE

1290-1335 T/D
- CHRISTIANS RECEIVE HOLPEN & MARTYRED
- MARTYRS OF CHRIST NOW "REFINED"
- MARTYRS GATHERED FROM THE SKY
- BLESSED IS HE WHO COMES TO THE 1335 DAYS. THIS IS THE WEDDING IN HEAVEN, THE MARRIAGE SUPPER OF THE LAMB. Note this is not the Kings Feast where the Bad and the Good are taken just prior to Armageddon.

© 2014–2018 © November 16, 2018 RICHARD VANDERPLOEG

TIME OF REDEMPTION
1260 DAYS

REDEEMED - REPENTED - SAVED
7 SPIRITS
7 THUNDERS
2 WITNESSES OF GOD
FLYING HELL MONSTERS
1040 T/D

- TEMPLE OF GOD, people worshiping there, but no Ark of God's Covenant present.

1290 T/D
- REDEEMED ISRAELITES "PRIOR TO SEEING" the abomination of desolation" in the Dragons temple 1290 T/d certain Israelites went to the Two Witnesses of God and accepted their Testimony "IN FAITH" they go to the "Wilderness Sanctuary" as the "Temple Priests"

1290-1400 T/D
- REPENTED ISRAELITES "AFTER SEEING" "abomination of desolation" 1290 T/d. Jesus said those in Judea flee to the hills. Certain Israelites flee and accepted their Testimony and go to the "Wilderness Sanctuary" as the "Repented Congregation".

1400-2300 T/D
- REPENTED SAVED NATIONS
Lands of the 10 kings. They accepted the Two Witnesses "Baptism unto Repentance," received and kept their salvation garments. They are the GOOD GUESTS in the KINGS WEDDING FEAST in the KINGS HALL.

2300 T/D
(Armageddon Countdown) A/C@-220 days

2300 - 2303.5 T/D Events

- SANCTUARY IS CLEANSED, now the Temple of God is seen having the Ark of His Covenant.
- GREAT RED DRAGON RELEASED
- TWO WITNESSES KILLED
- GOD'S COMMANDS:
  - "COME OUT OF HER MY PEOPLE"
  - "GO AND GATHER THE BAD & GOOD" for the natural feast so GOD'S WEDDING HALL may be filled with GUESTS. The 'bad' are evil seeds who repented out of fear and who are intended for the 1000-Year Kingdom (Gog included)
- DEMONS RELEASED, 200 million demons released from the Great Euphrates River now fly to Pakistan-India border and merge with 200 million 3-color zombies, transforming them into the "Entities of Death that now begin their 150 days of slaughter across the middle east and herding all 1-color zombies towards the dried up Great Euphrates River, for the great slaughter to the joy of the Great Red Dragon ++
- TWO WITNESSES RESURRECTED 3.5 days later at the 2303.5 T/D
- SATAN'S TEMPLE DESTROYED BY FIRE and crumbles into oblivion.

GREAT BABYLON DESTROYED
ARMAGEDDON

BOOKS 1-5 ₊₁

CONTENTS

Chapter One

MARRIAGE SUPPER

Maria, Joseph and Thomas, their time now concluded upon earth, rejoined their brethren and all rejoiced as the Marriage Supper commenced on the 1335th day in Heaven during the Great Tribulation.

Revelation 19:9-10   THE MARRIAGE SUPPER[1]
"Then he said to me,
'Blessed are those who are called to the **MARRIAGE SUPPER** *of the Lamb!'"*
And he said to me,
"These are the true sayings of God."

Daniel 12:12-13 PROPHECY OF THE END TIME
12 Blessed is he who waits, and comes to the **one thousand three hundred and thirty-five days**.
13 "But you, go your way till the end; for you shall rest, and will arise to your inheritance at the end of the days."
"Blessed is he who waits,
and comes to the one thousand three hundred and thirty-five days."
(1335 days)

Now, for some reason unknown to the three of them, they were given detailed knowledge of the events of the Wedding Ceremony that had already taken place prior to their Martyrdom. They saw the Bride, now Wife, and how radiant she looked. She looked at them in a loving way, and they knew that she already knew the three of them. They had many questions to ask her.

Mel, now waving to them one last time in his customary fashion, raised his hands in praise as his countenance grew to immense brilliance, and vanished.

Maria was relieved to feel that they were finally home. She smiled contently, but after what seemed only like a second later, gasped and said, "Oh no . . . where's Joe?"

Tom replied, "Oh no . . . here comes Mel, and he has Joe in tow."

"Oh no... What's happened?" she sighed exasperatingly.

"The Great Red Dragon is out of his pit!" shouted Joe.

"Joe... Joe... now what did you do?" Maria asked in an elevated voice.

Mel calmed her down, "It's alright, he didn't do it. I need you three to come with me, to the beginning of the 1000-year Kingdom and ending with Judgment Day.

Maria sighed, and Joe said, "You mean 'back to the future'."

The release of their built-up tension was overwhelming as all three bursts into uncontrolled hysterics.

"What's so funny? This is serious. You three have one last mission." Mel said, looking confused.

"Seems like we've heard that line before!" howled Maria.

Joe continued, "So we're going to 1000-year Kingdom and ending with Judgment Day. Mel, when this is over can you take us back, say five years, so I can get a book deal like Tom did?"

Mel sighed and said, "The things I do for 'King and Country'".

"Sure, now he quotes the legendary James Bond," said Joe.

Maria quipped, "Joe, James Bond is only a fictional character, just like you, right Mel?"

Mel looked at them with a strange expression then said cryptically, "The answer is written in

'THE EXODUS PROTOCOL.'"

"What's that?" Joe puzzlingly asked.

"Why, it's your book!" replied Mel.

Maria added, "Is Joe going to write a book?"

"It's already written, just not published," was his reply. The three looked confused, so he added, "Sometimes it's better to keep certain sad secrets sealed because they could create more-bad than good and alter timelines."

Joe lamented saying, "So I wrote a phantom book, too revealing to be published?"

Maria questioned Mel, "Can you elaborate a little further?"

Mel said, "Let's just say that there's a lot more to you three than you know. Remember, 'weigh me the weight of fire'".

Joe chuckling and rolling his eyes, replied, "I just love cryptic timeline shifting."

Maria, for the first time, decided to push Mel for a better answer.

Mel was pleased that they showed such an interest in God's plan for them. He said, "All three of you received the 3 Holy Sacraments when you were babies".

Joe had to ask, "Why didn't we know about this earlier in our lives, we may not have had to be martyred for our faith, and taken in the Rapture?"

Mel replied, "Think back, where did you just come from?"

Maria answered, "The Marriage Supper. But I still don't get it, I'm so confused."

Mel smiled and said, "Maria, Joe and Tom, what event preceded you being in the Marriage Supper?

They pondered his question for a moment, then Joe said, "We were martyred."

"Think harder." interjected Mel.

Then it dawned upon them and all three simultaneously answered; "Holpen".

Mel was pleased. "Yes, 'Holpen'! Now you are about to learn the full scope of what 'Holpen' is all about. Not only <u>did you not experience pain</u> *and* <u>trauma during your Martyrdom</u>, remember that calmness that came over you, that was My Hand touching your soul. Instantaneously, even before your dead bodies touched the ground, you were in the "Marriage Supper". Remember your very next thoughts, what were they?"

Maria, nodding, said, "A feeling of euphoria and Holy Awe and then joined by our loved ones."

"Yes," replied Mel, "and then what?"

"We were given special White Robes that had golden stripes and insignias down the right side."

"Now", Mel guided them further, "what were your robes made of? "

"Pure, white and fine, linen." Maria replied.

"Exactly," said Mel, "and what do these special garments signify?"

Joe perked up, "The righteous act of the saints!"

"Right again." Mel smiled. "You have just answered your previous question and now look at those golden lines and insignias."

All three were now able to read their insignias. Tom, paraphrasing, spoke first. "These insignias tell our history, it says we came out of the great tribulation, washed our robes and made them white in the blood of the Lamb. We also have palm branches in our hands signifying that our souls are at peace."

Maria added, "And I will paraphrase, as recorded in the Bible, we sing the praises, *Salvation belongs to our God who sits on the throne, and to the Lamb! And we are now Temple Priests serving before the throne of God. We serve Him day and night in His temple. And He who sits on the throne and dwells amongst us. We shall neither hunger nor thirst anymore; the sun shall not strike us, nor any heat; for the Lamb who is in the midst of the throne will shepherd us and lead us to living fountains of waters. And God has wiped away every tear from our eyes. "*

"Exactly." Mel commented, "You're 'Temple Priests'. And you are like Mary, Martha's sister, whose fame is eternal in the Bible." All three humbly bowed not knowing what to say or do next.

Leave it to Joe to break the tension by piping in, "Ok, let's get moving! I've got a book deal pending and as someone once said, I just love cryptic timeline shifting!"

The roar of silence was deafening; however, Joe didn't get it until Maria jabbed him saying, "It was you who said it, Joe! Silly!"

Unphased, he shrugged and rubbed his hands together. He was ready for their next mission. "Tom, make sure you bring a pad of paper and a pen. Let's play hard ball for that book deal. And we're going to have to watch the fine print for sure."

Mel's voice in the background, softly whispered, "Joe, I think we're going to have to redefine the definition of 'Temple Priests'".

Joe thought that was a compliment and smiled.

Mel remonstrated saying, "Really Joe?" he looked upward, "Give me patience, Lord."

Maria segued in asking; "Mel, what's the difference between 'Temple' and 'Tabernacle',

Before he could answer, Joe said, "The 'Temple'? Is that the area where the Temple Priests dwell within the New Jerusalem? And the 'Tabernacle' is that area where the soles of God's feet touch the ground."

Maria stared at Joe saying, "Where did you get this information?"

Joe replied, "What information?"

Mel smiled and said, "Let's move on."

CHAPTER TWO:

THE CATEGORIES

Mel reviewed the following categories all have at this time, the three Holy Sacraments.

1	Royal Kings of God	(RAPTURE)	Firstlings	Lord's Wife
2	Royal Priests of God	(RAPTURE)	Firstlings	Lord's Wife
3	Eternity Redeemed	(RAPTURE)	Overcomers	Priests
4	Wilderness Sanctuary	(1260 DAYS)	Overcomers	Priests
5	Martyrs of Understanding	(1335 GTP)	Great Tribulation	Priests
6	Martyrs of Christ, Testifiers	(1335 GTP)	Overcomers	Priests
7	Martyrs of Christ, Temple	(1335 GTP)	Overcomers	Priests

Tom told the other two, "We are from the #7 group, 'Temple Priests' martyred during the Great Tribulation time."

Joe added, "And from where the Temple Priests dwell, in the New Jerusalem."

Maria asked; "Does the order represent different levels of purity?"

Mel's answer was blunt and to the point, "'Purity is purity', there are no degrees. However, some will have increased scope such as the Royal Kings and Royal Priests. Maria, just be thankful you are included, remember God said, 'many are called but few are chosen'."

And also, remember the Prophet Daniel said, 'Blessed is he who waits, and comes to the one thousand three hundred and thirty-five days", (1335). "This includes you last three Martyrs of Christ."

"See the Bridegroom unveiled His Firstlings clothed with the Overcomers' bright and fine linen garments to all in attendance for the Marriage Supper. 'Behold my Wife'". Mel paused, the three marveled as his words resounded throughout Heaven like a thunderclap.

Maria said, "Yes, we are the last three prior to the appointed time of 1335 T/d. And yes, we are thankful for God's great love unto us. But what I'm asking is for you to please elaborate upon what is meant by 'The New Jerusalem' and 'The Lord's Wife'[2] as it pertains to the Firstlings and Overcomers."

Mel smiled, and answered, "The New Jerusalem, adorned as a Bride, is God's Holy City that comes down from Heaven unto earth. And in it only God, His Son and His Wife are its embodiment. I will describe the New Jerusalem in great detail a little later."

Joe replied ok but, "How can a city be a Bride?"

"Not a Bride Joe," Mel continued, "Wife, as she was adorned as a Bride".

Joe replied, "Just great. A riddle in a riddle. What's really the difference between the two?"

Mel answered, "Well now Joe, think back to when you first met Maria, what was the first step called in your relationship?"

Joe pondered for a few seconds, then said, "Girlfriend, I guess?"

"Right! And did this automatically mean that Maria would become your fiancé, and then your Bride?" Joe shook his head, and Mel continued, "Likewise, not all Brides mature into Wives, it is not a-given, remember the 5 foolish virgins Joe?"

Joe smirked, looked at Maria and said, "I can't remember dating that many." Maria gave him a wink. Once again, Mel had that 'weird or what' expression on his face.

Mel continued, "The Lord's Wife, as it pertains to the Firstlings and Overcomers, is found in Revelation 19:6. I will paraphrase it for you... *"For the marriage of the Lamb has come, and His wife has made herself ready."*

These are the Firstlings.

"Next, our Lord's Wife was adorned and arrayed in fine linen, clean and bright, for the fine linen is the righteous acts of the saints. These represent the combined Godly acts of those who lived morally correct and God-fearing lives, the Overcomers." Mel explained.

These are the Overcomers.

Mel continued, "The Wife is clothed with these overcomers, so you see that she comprises the seven categories as shown above. Easy for some, impossible for others to comprehend."

"Mel could you elaborate further exactly what you mean by the word 'Firstling'?" Maria asked.

"Of course. They excelled well past what was expected of them. One thing is for sure, the Lamb's Wife is comprised of many components, all forming part of the whole, and all having a go forward function. The Royal Kings and Royal Priests of God, and perhaps you three have a Galactic Quest".

"Great! Another book title!" segued Joe, who was fully prepared for another Heavenly rib poke. However, almost to his chagrin, nothing happened, and he thought he must be losing his touch.

Tom whispered, "That's the second-time Mel alluded to us having more involvement in addition to being Temple Priests."

CHAPTER THREE:

MARRIAGE FEAST

Matthew 22:10

THE MARRIAGE FEAST, in the
MARRIAGE (KINGS) HALL AND THE
BAD & GOOD GUESTS

10 So those servants went out into the highways and gathered
together all whom they found,

*both **BAD***

*and **GOOD**.*

And the Marriage hall was filled with guests.

Mel said, "Remember a while back during the Great Tribulation at the 2300 T/D., when the Temple is Cleansed? At this time, the 'Saved' are gathered by God's Angels in what you called those massive starships and brought into the MARRIAGE (KINGS) HALL for the MARRIAGE FEAST OF THE LAMB. As you said, this was fantastic. Just as in Marriage feasts of times past, there was a head-table of sorts, guests, and many other items. Somehow, everyone was transported into their respective groups. The strange thing was that everyone had the exact same view, none were closer or farther, none were in the center nor on the outer fringes, all were one.

Remember when Tom delved into the definitions of 'called' and 'chosen.' A definition or synonym for 'called' is Baptized or Christened, while a definition of 'chosen' is 'one who is the focus of Divine Favor.'

God draws His chosen, to His Son. We read in John 6:44, Jesus said, 'No one can come to Me unless the Father who sent Me, draws him."

Also, in John 14:6. 6, Jesus said to him, "I am the way, the truth, and the life. No one comes to the Father except through Me."

So, who are the 'called' and 'chosen' in the Marriage Hall? Let's keep going.

In Revelation 22:10-11, *and he said to me, 'Do not seal the words of the prophecy of his book, for the time is at hand. He who is unjust, let him be unjust still; he who is filthy, let him be filthy still; he who is righteous, let him be righteous still; he who is holy, let him be holy still.'*

Now let's just restate these four groups and then analyze them.

He who is unjust…	let him be unjust still
He who is filthy…	let him be filthy still
He who is righteous…	let him be righteous still
He who is holy…	let him be holy still

In these four categories, see that the first two are evil and it may appear strange that in God's Marriage Hall (where the Feast for His Son and Wife now takes place) that evil would still be present at this late stage of redemption, just bear in mind 'evil-seeds'."

Mel gave them a moment to reflect on all the information and review what they had just been told. Joe stretched, and said, "It seems like we are here, to report on the events that transpire during this Feast."

"And so much more." added Mel. "There are two good groups, the Righteous and the Holy. The Righteous are those who lived a morally correct and God-fearing life, from times past and the Great Tribulation time, that includes you three."

Maria mused aloud, "I don't recall being righteous, just normal."

Mel continued, "Normal is good. The Holy, are those of Divine Origin and have been Consecrated to God. They are the 'Holy Children of God', 'chosen' by God as the 'Bride' for His Son who through grace, then matured into the Wife. You may ask why the difference between the two last groups? During their lives on earth, the 'Righteous' have 2-Sacraments and the 'Holy' have 3-Sacraments.

As to why? As the Archangel Gabriel said to Daniel, 'He believed,' meaning some thought it necessary to obtain the three Sacraments, while others were content with two."

Tom asked; "What about Christians who did not know that the three Holy Sacraments even existed?"

Mel just smiled saying, "We read in, Matthew 22:14 *'For many are called, but few are chosen.'* Don't worry, all will in due time have the opportunity for salvation."

Maria, somewhat perplexed, questioned; "It seems like we three had the 3 Holy Sacraments and yet turned out to be the last three Martyrs of Christ. How can this really happen?

Mel replied, "That's why you three are different and please don't push for a more detailed answer, at least for now that is."

Maria acquiesced. "For now." she whispered as she softly sighed.

CHAPTER FOUR:

SATAN IN THE MARRIAGE (KINGS) HALL

Maria was commenting how it still made her feel somewhat eerie to see chairs above her, which she thought looked sort of like many balconies layered upon each other. "This dimension thing is fascinating, yet a little weird to get used to. But by concentrating, I can sort of block them out and just focus on the center table. You know, I am kind of here and there. Whoa! I almost said, 'weird or what'. Maybe I shouldn't use this phrase any longer."

Joe, oblivious to her last comment, pointed to the food on the tables and said, "Hey that's weird, never thought I'd see that."

Maria nodded, "Now who would have thought that real food would be here?"

Joe said, "But sure it makes sense. Why not? There are many millions of the 'Saved' people still in their physical bodies that were recently gathered by God's Angels and brought here."

Tom made a casual remark, "Look at the vast numbers gathered; I wonder how many people will survive Judgment Day?"

Joe added, "Or be deleted."

Maria said, "Now that saddens me to think people will still reject our Heavenly Father's Love. Hopefully, this current number decreases exponentially. This a strange one. Here we have a most glorious event and guess who pops in for dinner? One might ask, 'How did he get in and why was he there?'"

Mel simply said, "As to the how, Satan, the evil one, was not challenged when he entered into the Marriage Hall. The Angels and God knew he was there, and all knew he did not have a Marriage garment."

They all simultaneously thought the same thought, "Why?" and then all immediately answered their own thoughts with "He's only there observing his 'evil seeds'."

Tom looked around then asked, "Why can't we identify these evil-hearted people?"

Mel replied, "You can't but God can. And remember that evil dwells within, not all consider themselves evil, and outward appearances can be deceiving. Remember the 'wolf in sheep's clothing'. Now keep silent and view what takes place next."

As God entered the hall, He immediately went to one not having a white Marriage garment. From their vantage point, they saw that God was talking to this person. It would be impossible to describe the appearance of God even looking through their eyes, just yet.

"Strange." Maria whispered, "God is not yelling at him, it seems more like pity."

Mel whispered back, "Who wants to see their creation disintegrating into oblivion? Remember that Angels have free will, and some were persuaded to follow 'pride and abandoned love'." If they only would have had faith in their God, they would have witnessed a most spectacular creation and would have been part of it. Instead, pride got in their way and they have been in torment ever since."

Maria asked, "Can these fallen angels repent, and return to God?"

"Not possible." Mel sighed and added, "Now watch what takes place next."

The three of them knew to whom God was talking.

Tom said, "Look, Angels restrained and bound Satan using supernatural means! And upon God's command, they cast him out of the Wedding Hall, and into blackness!"

Maria commented, "Into 'outer darkness' is what the Bible calls it."

Mel said, "This means he was cast into a state known as hell or to put it another way, an existence void of God. Satan was now cast out of the king's hall and back to the hell on earth, for at this time the Battle of Armageddon has not yet taken place, yet it is at hand.

Did you notice Satan was speechless before the Almighty God who says, '*Bind him hand and foot, take him away, and cast him into outer darkness, there will be weeping and gnashing of teeth.' For many are called, but few are chosen?*"

Maria said, "There is that saying again: '*For many are called, but few are chosen*'." Many in the Marriage hall are called but oh so many will fail during the 1000-Year Kingdom."

Mel refocused them by saying, "Let's now look at what happens when God said, *"Many are called but few are chosen."*

CHAPTER FIVE:

PURPOSE OF THE 1000-YEARS

In a great second, the three now began observing their surroundings, only this time with all memories of their lives, now crystal clear. They thought it was amazing and found themselves travelling and witnessing once again, the good, the bad and as Joe added, "the ugly" everyone just ignored him (as usual).

Mel began by saying, "Remember prior to Armageddon, many of the 'good' and some of the 'bad' living upon the earth either accepted or acquiesced to the Testimony of the Two Witnesses of God, and received their 'Baptism unto Repentance'. They were given 'Marriage Garments', were instructed to keep them clean, and were allowed to participate in the King's Feast. They came from the 'Time of Redemption' during the Great Tribulation and prior to Armageddon.

The 1000-Year time-period is for the 'saved' to prove to their God that they are deserving of His Love and not turn away from Him over time.

It is recorded in scripture that 'A new nation is born in one day; these are the above <u>Guests in the Marriage Hall for the Kings Feast.</u>' They are the repented people from the 'saved nations' formerly of the 10 kings, save and except the 'evil-seeds', whose importance we will discuss soon.

<u>In addition, there will arise another nation, an Army that comes up out of the ground and comes back to life also in one day</u>, I will also discuss them soon. They form the Citizens of the Kingdom of Peace verses those who turn away and form the anti-God along

with the evil-seeds, who only have no peace. Revelation 3:18 says, *'I counsel you to buy from Me gold refined in the fire, that you may be rich; and white garments, that you may be clothed, that the shame of your nakedness may not be revealed; and anoint your eyes with eye salve, that you may see.'*

Remember it is recorded in Revelation 3:5 *'He who overcomes shall be clothed in white garments, and I will not blot out his name from the Book of Life; but I will confess his name before My Father and before His angels.* This means their names are erased from the Judgment Day books and entered into the Book of Life, meaning they will live eternally as citizens."

Mel continued, "There are various categories of souls upon the earth during the 1000-Year Kingdom. It is necessary to have some background information to see where they came from and what their roles are.

The most spectacular group came from the efforts of Jesus, God's Son who made it possible for humans to come back to God. Now, having said this, what did Jesus do that was so spectacular?"

CHAPTER SIX:

JESUS AND HIS MINISTRY

Mel began, "This chapter details certain groups of souls existing during the 1000-Years and gives background information to the reader. Some may consider it too laborious while others will find it fascinating."

Joe commented, "Seems like it's going to be a lot of information to digest, perhaps more than my attention span that is limited to 5 minutes of reading at one time."

Mel concluded with, "Lump of coal or diamond."

Joe, not really grasping the comment, then added, "You know, coal turns into a diamond."

Maria just had to contribute, "Yes but it takes a million years to do so, however this didn't seem to resonate with Joe who thought it was some type of compliment."

Mel continued, "The following is a lot of background-information, so if your attention span is limited to only 5 minutes like Joe's, you may simply skip over it, for now.

Following Jesus Baptism by John the Baptist, we read in Matthew 4: 1-11 *"Jesus lead by the Spirit into the wilderness to be tempted by the devil. After fasting for 40 days he was then tempted"*.

After the 40 days, we read in Matthew 4:12-16 *Now when Jesus heard that John had been put in prison, He departed to Galilee. And leaving Nazareth, He came and dwelt in Capernaum, which is by the sea, in the regions of Zebulun and Naphtali, that it might be fulfilled which was spoken by Isaiah the prophet, saying: "The land of Zebulun and the land of Naphtali, by the way of the sea, beyond the Jordan,*

Galilee of the Gentiles:" The people who sat in darkness have seen a great light, And upon those who sat in the region and shadow of death, Light has dawned. "

Matthew 4:17 From that time Jesus began to preach and to say, **"Repent, for the kingdom of heaven is at hand. "**

DIFFERENCE BETWEEN THE BAPTISM OF JOHN AND JESUS

John baptized with water unto repentance.

Paul affirms this in Acts 19:4: *"John's baptism was a baptism of repentance. He told the people to believe in the one coming after him, that is, in Jesus. "*

> *Jesus said, "Most assuredly, I say to you,*
> *unless one is born of **water** and the **Spirit**,*
> *he cannot enter the kingdom of God. John 3:5*

This is done in the name of God the Father, God the Son and God the Holy Spirit. This Holy Act is tied to the death, burial, and resurrection of Christ and due to the sacrifice on the cross by Jesus, it completely washes away the sins of the forefathers.

Our Lord's Holy Baptism with Water allows the believer to become a friend of God. All claims of and from the past deeds from Adam till now, are made null and void. There is an old saying 'his grandfather was a thief; his father was a thief and now his son follows in his footsteps'. For example, when the people wanted to kill Jesus they cried out as recorded in Matthew 27:25 *'and all the people answered and said, 'His blood be on us and on our children'.* This means they were prepared to have a curse put upon them and their children in order to have Jesus crucified. It is no wonder that Jesus said to his Father as recorded in, Luke 23:34 NKJV *Then Jesus said, "Father, forgive them, for they do not know what they do. "*

Ponder this, how do curses manifest themselves upon humans? Evil spirits and demons can lay claim to people and possess them making them their puppets to carry out murderous acts.

Our Lord's Holy Baptism with Water nullified all claims by evil entities of the past possessing humans. Remember people in the

Bible who had demons possessing them, were cast out by Jesus or his Apostles. Even today people talk about living past lives complete with past memories. They call this reincarnation, when in fact it is simply these spirits possessing their minds for their own agenda. There are many deceiving demons and spirits hell-bent on possessing people to carry out horrendous acts of violence and then taking these duped souls to hell with them. People have a saying, 'The devil made me do it.' Don't dismiss their comments as meaningless garble. Remember Satan is god of this earth and all people are heathens until Baptized with Water in the name of the Holy Trinity.

HOLY BAPTISM WITH THE HOLY SPIRIT
Jesus commissioned his twelve disciples/Apostles.

And when He had called His twelve disciples to Him, He gave them power over unclean spirits, to cast them out, and to heal all kinds of sickness and all kinds of disease.

Mel commented, "That the Son of God's sacrifice rested solely upon His work continuing upon earth. Jesus entrusted His work of salvation that he initiated into the hands of His Apostles having as their leader the Apostle Peter known as the rock. I previously stated this passage however it bears repeating.

Jesus commissions His Apostles to Baptize with the Holy Spirit.

The following are some references to the Apostles.

Ephesians 4:11 New King James Version (NKJV) And He Himself gave some to be apostles, some prophets, some evangelists, and some pastors and teachers,

Acts 2:42 And they continued steadfastly in the apostles' doctrine and fellowship, in the breaking of bread, and in prayers.

Matthew 28: 18-20 18 And Jesus came and spoke to them, saying, "All authority has been given to Me in heaven and on earth. 19 Go therefore and make disciples of all the nations, baptizing them in the name of the Father and of the Son and of the Holy Spirit, 20 teaching them to observe all things that I have commanded you; and lo, I am with you always, even to the end of the age." Amen.

Tom asked, "We just read above, that the Apostles baptized in the name of the Father and of the Son and of the Holy Spirit and recently you told us of the 3 Holy Sacraments, please again explain what it meant by this."

Mel elaborated, "Yes there are <u>3 Holy Sacraments</u>, the first is the Holy Baptism with Water, next the Holy Communion, and then the Baptism with the Holy Spirit. Jesus said to His Apostles

Most assuredly,
I say to you, unless one is born of water and the Spirit,
he cannot enter the kingdom of God.
John 3:5

"Note, it says unless one is born of water and the Spirit, he cannot enter the kingdom of God. It does not say that they cannot enter into various realms, some good, many not so good."

Remember Jesus said, in John 14:2-4

In My Father's house are many mansions; if it were not so, I would have told you. I go to prepare a place for you. 3 And if I go and prepare a place for you, I will come again and receive you to Myself; that where I am, there you may be also. 4 And where I go you know, and the way you know."

Mel added, "See, there are many mansions, meaning 'large dwelling places'. The Son of God though, is preparing a place for those reborn of Water and the Spirit and there, He resides."

Now continuing, "He clarified the difference between the Water Baptism and the Baptism with the Holy Spirit in Acts 8: 14-17.

14, Now when the apostles who were at Jerusalem heard that Samaria had received the word of God, they sent Peter and John to them, 15 who, when they had come down, prayed for them that they might receive the Holy Spirit. 16 For as yet He had fallen upon none of them. They had only been baptized in the name of the Lord Jesus. 17 Then they laid hands on them, and they received the Holy Spirit.

They had only been baptized in the name of the Lord Jesus.
(This is the Water Baptism)
Then they laid hands on them, and they received the Holy Spirit.
(This is the Holy Spirit Baptism)

Mel concluded by saying, "See, these are the two Baptisms, and also Jesus instructed His Apostles to forgive sins and the breaking of bread: Holy Communion.

If you are reading this book prior to the Rapture, when world rulers such as people in the United Nations say "Peace and Safety" look up for the Rapture is at hand.

Once again Jesus instructed his Apostle to preach,
"The Kingdom of Heaven is at hand".

CHAPTER SEVEN:

DESCRIPTION OF THE NEW JERUSALEM

Mel said, "Whether or not you have read the above chapter, let's move on. Joe, what does the Lambs 'Wife' look like?"

Joe replied saying, "She is God's Holy City, the New Jerusalem descending out of Heaven and radiating the Glory of God. Her light was like a most precious stone, like a jasper stone, clear as crystal. She is most spiritually spectacular to behold, and until one witnesses her totality, let's just say, Behold the Lamb's Wife."

Maria smiled thinking, "That's the perfect answer, I couldn't have expressed it any better myself." until she noticed Joe reading from the book, she acquiesced.

Mel looked at them and rhetorically commented, "The 'Wife' is clothed with the righteous acts of the saints, so you simply described yourself." The three looked at each other, were speechless yet thinking, "timeline shifting again." Mel said, "Instead of reading the following Bible verses Revelation 21: 1-27 I will just paraphrase them to accommodate Joe's limited attention span[3] detailing the Heavenly aspects of the New Jerusalem so people in another time frame can see what's coming soon."

Joe asked, "Who are those in another time frame?"

Mel smiled saying, "Remember, Joe, you three are timeline-shifting again. Those who may be reading will be in the time prior to the Rapture. We will read the following and then discuss them in depth. And Joe, pay attention to the following. I know it's a lot of reading but it's very important for those viewing through your eyes to read every word, for it is possible that they may be reading after the Rapture has taken place and then this book will be solace for them"

Mel looked at them and said, "Now let's begin paraphrasing Revelation 21: 1-27

Verse 1,
The continents have recombined, the great ocean surrounding the recombined land masses still exist as spoken of by God in Ezekiel 39:6 *'And I will send fire on Magog and <u>on those who live in security in the coastlands.'</u>*

Verse 3,
Behold, the tabernacle of God is with men, and He will dwell with them, and they shall be His people. God Himself will be with them and be their God. This sentence speaks for itself.

Verse 4,
<u>In God's holy mountain</u> there shall be no more death, nor sorrow, nor crying and there shall be no more pain. *(And God will wipe away every tear from their eyes; there shall be no more death, nor sorrow, nor crying. There shall be no more pain, for the former things have passed away.")*

Within the New Jerusalem there will be PEACE, no death, sorrow, crying or pain.

Now as to the areas of Gog and his Magog nations who live outside of the New Jerusalem, that's a different story, I will explain them later on.

Verse 6,
I will give of the fountain of the water of life freely to him who thirsts. This is given to those who remain loyal to God, as to the evil-others, that's a different story.

Verse 21,
The twelve gates were twelve pearls: each individual gate was of one pearl. Now imagine a pearl the size of a gate. Pearls glisten from the light emanating from the Holy City. 'And the streets of the city were

pure gold, like transparent glass.' 'As to the twelve gates I will discuss their relevance soon.'

Verse 23,
The city had no need of the sun or of the moon to shine in it, for the glory of God illuminated it. <u>See, God's Glory illuminated the city.</u>

Verse 24-26,
And the nations of those who are saved shall walk in its light. The New Jerusalem radiates God's Glory through the 12 pearly gates and from above its high walls. Those loyal to God who surround the New Jerusalem bask in this Glorious light, they have no need for the sun or moons light.

<u>The kings</u> shall bring the glory and the honor of the nations into it. *But there shall by no means enter it anything that defiles, or causes an abomination or a lie, <u>but only those who are written in the</u> <u>Lamb's Book of Life</u>.*

Note: only those reborn with the Water and Holy Spirit Baptisms dwell within the New Jerusalem.

Now you can see that the **Royal Kings of God** who travel throughout the lands of the 12 Tribes, and the nations surrounding them, can bring the 'Honor of the Nations' into the New Jerusalem. These kings are those whose names are written in the **Lamb's Book of Life**; remember **they are the Firstlings**."

Joe asked about the importance of the 12 pearly gates, to which Mel replied, "I will discuss them soon my friend, soon."

Tom added, "We could refer to the street as transparent gold, even though this material is not found on earth."

Mel continued, "The Glory of the New Jerusalem. <u>God and His Son are the temple</u> illuminated by God's Glory and the Lamb is its light, remember the words spoken a long time ago, 'I am the light of the world.' "

Mel once again in his customary fashion waived his arm and time-line-shifting commenced.

CHAPTER EIGHT:

THE NEW JERUSALEM
DESCENDS UNTO EARTH

With a "wiggle in time" they found themselves observing the New Jerusalem descending out of Heaven.

Mel now turned his attention to the dimensions of the New Jerusalem saying, "Consider this, the walls of the city are 1400 hundred miles on each of its four sides. Its walls are over 200 feet high and each side has three gates of entry.

"Joe, answer me this question, since the city has equal widths and height and comes down from Heaven, does it come <u>unto earth</u>, <u>onto earth</u> or <u>into the earth</u>, what does this mean?"

Joe confused said, "I don't really think there is any difference between <u>unto earth</u>, <u>onto earth</u> or <u>into the earth</u>?"

"Not so fast," replied Mel. "First consider this, if such a vast city were to touch the earth's surface and since the earth is curved, would it sit flat or would it be higher at each end and wobble like a teeter-totter?"

Joe still confused pondered and said, "If the walls of the great city rested upon the earth and since the earth is curved," and doing some quick math, continued, "then the walls would have to be over 1000 feet high at each corner to be able to be 200 feet in the middle. So, either there are massive end supports on its four corners or the 200 feet high walls curve to the surface of the earth or something else takes place."

Mel continued, "See, it's huge being the size roughly half the size of your nation and that's only its ground floor, remember its 1400 miles high."

"I get it." replied Joe. "The answer lies somewhere in the wordings, <u>unto earth</u>, <u>onto earth</u> or <u>into the earth</u>."

"That's correct," responded Mel.

Joe, now flummoxed, lamented, "If I'm correct, why don't I understand my answer, please explain the difference to me, because I really don't get it."

Maria segued Mel's question, asking, "Why is the New Jerusalem so high?" Mel's answer was weird… smilingly he whispered… "Large family, and God leaves none behind, they are with Him Eternally. Remember Jesus once said that in His Father's House were many mansions, meaning many large dwelling places."

Joe attempted to compute the total volume of this city and quickly gave up saying, "The possibilities are endless as to how many beings, animals and who knows what else, can live within the New Jerusalem."

Tom added, "Try to imagine 1400 miles high and today the clouds closest to the earth are about one-mile-high, so if each level was one-mile-high this would come to at least 1,400 levels and as Joe said, the possibilities are endless … it boggles the imagination."

Joe commented, "A structure so high extending into space would cause the earth to wobble, so how is this effect compensated?"

Now all looked up and watched again as the New Jerusalem descended.

Joe said, "See it's tethered not separate, but still part of the whole."

Maria added, "Look, it's almost touching the surface of the earth . . . now that's weird, never imagined that happening.

Tom yelled out, "Tell me about it." Now all witnessed something miraculous.

Joe pointed out something they had completely missed before. The Angel talking to the Apostle John had a measuring stick and measured the height of the walls and everything <u>but</u> the 12 foundations of the New Jerusalem. Now they knew why.

These 12 foundations were sufficiently high enough to rest not only on but settled into the earth making the New Jerusalem perfectly level. All topographical variations in land or water elevations were nullified. Joe added, "Wow! The New Jerusalem did all three, it came from Heaven, <u>unto, onto</u> and then <u>into the earth</u>'.

Mel began to describe these massive 12 foundations of different colors. *Now the walls of the city had twelve foundations, and on them were the names of the twelve apostles of the Lamb. 15 And he who talked with me had a gold reed to measure the city, its gates, and its wall.*

19 The foundations of the wall of the city were adorned with all kinds of precious stones: the first foundation was jasper, the second sapphire, the third chalcedony, the fourth emerald, 20 the fifth sardonyx, the sixth sardius, the seventh chrysolite, the eighth beryl, the ninth topaz, the tenth chrysoprase, the eleventh jacinth, and the twelfth amethyst.

24 <u>And the nations of those who are saved shall walk in its light, and the kings of the earth bring their glory and honor into it.</u>

25 Its gates shall not be shut at all by day (there shall be no night there).

26 And they shall bring the glory and the honor of the nations into it.

27 <u>But there shall by no means enter it anything that defiles, or causes an abomination or a lie, but only those who are written in the Lamb's Book of Life.</u>

Mel continued, "Up to now we've been discussing the physical attributes of the New Jerusalem, now you are witnessing the complexities of its interdimensional attributes."

Joe said, "I don't have a clue what that means."

Mel simply replied, "Don't try to figure it out, just accept it."

Tom added, "It's really...really huge." The tethering makes it look like a triangle and God's Holy mountain fits into it perfectly. The mountain is enormously high, and it extends outwards in massive plateaus that are perfect for farming and all this is within its four walls."

Maria commented, "God's Holy Mountain reaches upwards, tethered by dazzling light. The only words able to describe this spectacular sight in a way that the human mind can comprehend is 'awestruck'." Heaven itself is far more massive and encompasses the Holy City itself being massive,"

Tom asked, "Could you please give us more information, what does it mean, 'and the kings of the earth bring their glory and honor into it?'"

Mel replied, "Now that's a question that defines God's plan of salvation to a tee. The kings are the Royal Kings of God, the first-lings who developed from God's people, to the Bride of His Son and further into His Son's Wife. This is Heaven's highest gift from God. The Royal Kings have the unique power of the 'rods of iron', vastly powerful energy weapons that keep the anti-God at bay. You could refer to them as a type of force field device that can either shock people to panic and flee or much worse."

Mel continued to talk about the Royal Kings and Royal Priests:

Revelation 1:6 *To Him who loved us and washed us from our sins in His own blood, and has made us <u>kings and priests</u> to His God and Father, to Him be glory and dominion forever and ever. Amen.*

1 Peter 2:9 But you are a chosen generation, <u>a royal priesthood</u>, a holy nation, His own special people, that you may proclaim the praises of Him who called you out of darkness into His marvelous light

Revelation 2: 27 'He shall rule them with a <u>rod of iron</u>; They shall be dashed to pieces like the potter's vessels' as I also have received from My Father

Psalm 2:9
You shall break them with a <u>rod of iron</u>; You shall dash them to pieces like a potter's vessel.
Revelation 2:27
'He shall rule them with a <u>rod of iron</u>; They shall be dashed to pieces like the potter's vessels' as I also have received from My Father.

Revelation 12:5
She bore a male Child who was to rule all nations with a <u>rod of iron</u>.
And her Child was caught up to God and His throne.

Revelation 19:15
Now out of His mouth goes a sharp sword, that with it He should strike
the nations. And He Himself will rule them with a <u>rod of iron</u>. He
Himself treads the winepress of the fierceness and wrath of Almighty
God.

Mel said, "Satan, now captured, as recorded in Revelation *20:*
1-3 (Then I saw an angel coming down from heaven, having the key
to the bottomless pit and a great chain in his hand. He laid hold of the
dragon, that serpent of old, who is the Devil and Satan, and bound him
for a thousand years; and he cast him into the bottomless pit, and shut
him up, and set a seal on him, so that he should deceive the nations no
more till the thousand years were finished. <u>But after these things he must</u>
<u>be released for a little while.</u>) is bound for 1000-Years, then released
for 15 months to rile up and gather his evil-seeds for the final battle
and Judgment Day."

CHAPTER NINE:

FUNCTIONALITY
OF GOD'S CHILDREN

el smiled, turning to the three heroes, and all other partakers in the feast of knowledge, and reiterating there is no so-called hierarchy, he again stressed that they are all 100% pure before God only their functionality and capacity differs.

THE ROYAL KINGS

'Firstlings' are taken in the Rapture and together with their exact counterparts in Eternity awaiting them, will rule with the 'rod of iron' and oversee the Holy Sacraments to the saved people of the nation's currently wearing their garments of salvation. Reference to the Royal Kings is recorded as follows. As it says in the Parable of the talents, they were given 5 talents and increased by 5 totaling 10. They were also given the one talent taken from the wicked and lazy servant. The Royal Kings therefore have 11 Talents. Their scope has the greatest capacity.

THE ROYAL PRIESTS

'Firstlings' are taken in the Rapture and together with their exact counterparts in Eternity awaiting them, will rule with the 'rod of iron' and dispense the Holy Sacraments to the saved people of the nation currently wearing their garments of salvation. They are also referenced in the Parable of the Talents; they were given 2 talents and increased them by 2 totaling 4. The Royal Priests have 4 Talents.

REFINED, CHILDREN OF GOD

'Overcomers' come from the Great Domed City (the Wilderness Sanctuary) who needed a little more time to mature and are taken up by the Lord to Heaven at the 1260 T/D. They received special fellowship during these days allowing them to mature. Remember, not all are the first fruits. Some fruits mature later; however, they're still good and form part of the harvest.

Maria spoke asking a question out of left-field. This Wilderness Sanctuary within the Great Domed City, who comprises them?

Mel smiled saying, "They consisted of those having the 3 and 2 Holy Baptisms. Should you be so inquisitive as to ask how many, let's just say hundreds of millions."

Joe commented, "What about sincere Godly pet lovers who cared for His creation?

Mel again smiled saying, "Yes, all of them and even more!'

The three were stunned by the enormity of this group within the Great Domed City.

Maria again commented, "The scope of God's plan of salvation is so massive and He truly desires all mankind to be saved."

Joe thought out loud saying, "After the Rapture took place and the Great Red Dragon (Satan) failed along with his fallen angels to defeat the forces of God, and to kill the Firstlings taken up to God in Heaven and again then failed to kill those transported to the "Great Domed City" he must have been in a rage when he went to persecute Christians left-behind who are referred to as 'the remnant of her seed'."

Sadly, Mel commented, "Those who turned their backs on the Son of God, chose poorly. They suffered the onslaught of evil, some amended their ways, received Holpen and were martyred for their belief in God, prior to the appointed time, and taken up but sadly others failed."

"Now, back to those in the Wilderness Sanctuary during these days, who do you think counselled them? Here is a hint. It says in Revelation 'where she is nourished for a time and times and half a time', that's 1260 days. If you said an angel counselled them, you are wrong, or the Two Witnesses of God, wrong again. It says 'nourished'. Do you think this only means 'food'? Think! Why are they in the Wilderness Sanctuary in the first place? They are there for additional spiritual nourishment that will enable them to mature, so who supplies this nourishment?"

"The answer is the Holy Spirit."

Maria smiled and said, "So those who in the past thought, what about my husband, wife or other loved ones, what if they're not quite ready, what is their fate if I'm taken, and they're not? Now they know the other side of the story. There will be no separation, for 'love' is eternal. They will rejoin their loved ones soon enough."

Joe interjected saying, "It's just the pecking order that is different, right Mel?"

Mel nodded saying, "That's one way of saying it. *Again, in Revelation we read, 'Rise and measure the temple of God, the altar, and those who worship there.'* Do you believe this altar is manmade of stones? It isn't. One last tidbit of information to read carefully for it says the 'temple of God'. This altar even though on earth is tethered to Heaven. Those in the Wilderness Sanctuary receive spiritual food and are connected to the congregation in Heaven. And since they are taken by our Lord into Heaven at the 1260 T/D this places them still within the timeframe of the Marriage Ceremony festivities, for the upcoming Marriage Supper does not commence until the 1335 T/d., as prophesied by the Prophet Daniel."

Tom commented, "I could never have fathomed such happenings. God's plan of salvation is like looking through the Hubble telescope, the deeper you see into the depths of the Universe, the more complicated it is."

Mel said, "Now we come to the next group, the

REFINED, CHILDREN OF GOD, MARTYRS OF UNDERSTANDING

These are the prodigal children of God who didn't fully comprehend God's Plan of Salvation or their function in it. Their opinions lead them in many directions. Unfortunately, they sidestepped the time of grace prior to the Rapture. Later, they saw and corrected their error and came home prior to the appointed time. Their intimate knowledge of their Heavenly Father's Plan of Salvation was now their foundation that supported their actions and gave them the courage to testify and lead Christians who were in a state of shock as to the circumstances they now found themselves in.

In the beginning, they rallied the Christians stealthily, and commencing with the Two Witnesses of God, these Martyrs of Understanding, declared open warfare upon the unholy trinity at the 1040 T/D. Their rallying actions ramped up exponentially, and their bold actions targeted themselves for death, mainly by beheading, in the eyes of the unholy trinity, prior to the 1260 T/d.

They were the first, during these last days, to be martyred. Their time of refinement now completed, they received 'Holpen'. The Martyrs of understanding, God's prodigal children were now home. They never denied their God, but they separated themselves from His love and simply lacked absolute conviction of faith in His plan of salvation.

I will give you a parable that explains them. Paraphrasing John 20:24-29 it says that after the resurrection of the Son of God, the Apostles of Christ were gathered together except the Apostle Thomas who days later came to them and when they told him that Jesus was in their midst he doubted their words saying 'Unless I see in His hands the print of the nails, and put my finger into the print of the nails, and put my hand into His side, I will not believe.'

Remember, Thomas was one of them, he was an Apostle, they all loved him but his doubt was greater than his belief. For eight days, he separated himself from the congregation.

Later Thomas was again with them and Jesus appeared to them, and to Thomas he said, 'reach your finger here, and look at My hands; and reach your hand here, and put it into My side'.

Jesus admonished him, 'Do not be unbelieving, but believing.' And Thomas answered and said to Him, 'My Lord and my God!' Jesus said to him, 'Thomas, because you have seen Me, you have believed. Blessed are those who have not seen and yet have believed.'"

Maria asked, "Why was he absent for eight days?"

Mel answered, "Some hear and believe while others require more proof."

Joe said, "Those living in the Rapture's aftermath, certainly now have their proof."

Tom added, "Thomas was not cast out of the congregation, he was loved. Jesus simply said, "You had to see to believe, blessed are they who have not seen, and yet have believed."

Joe asked, "So what became of Thomas?"

Mel replied and to his credit, "Thomas travelled great distances and did great works in the name of Christ."

Joe said, "That's reassuring to know, just like us?"

"No," Mel retorted, "When you three heard, you believed."

Curious, Maria asked, "Exactly when did we hear and believe?"

Mel smiled, "That's an answer your Bridegroom will give you. Let's finish with this group. Due to their absence, they miss the Rapture, and live during the Rapture's Aftermath; however, they go on to do great works in the name of Christ until their martyrdom. As Daniel said, it is still prior to the appointed time."

"Now we come to another group of Christians, the

REFINED, UNDER THE ALTAR MARTYRS #1 GROUP (Priests)

These souls are from the Dark Middle Ages. Not so long ago they were Baptized (sealed) with the Holy Spirit, the third Holy Sacrament in the eternal realms, as Tom mentions in this book and referred to as the Commencement date of the First Resurrection. Maria you were correct. They were not given 'palm branches, a sign of peace and reconciliation'. As recorded in Revelation 7:9, this group is ready to go into action during the Kingdom of Peace. It also says in Revelation 6:10-*11 that they were crying with a loud voice, saying, 'How long, O Lord until You judge and avenge our blood on those who dwell on the earth?'* Their pain of their martyrdom was now replaced with Holy Zeal and they're anxious to go forth as mighty testifiers of their Lord. They were told by Jesus to be patient for a little while until their fellow brethren were killed like they were and would come their way. The next group fulfilled the "fellow brethren" as I just stated, and were the conclusion of the First Resurrection that occurs during the Great Tribulation time.

Next are the

REFINED, GREAT TRIBULATION MARTYRS #2 GROUP (Temple Priests)

"Great Exploit Martyrs" 1290-1335 T/d.

They are recorded in Revelation 7:15 gathered from the sky at the sound of the great trumpet during the "Time of Refinement" Also recorded in Revelation 7:16 they are the Temple Priests who serve God. In Revelation, *7:17 it says God Himself will wipe away every tear from their eyes.* This is a most powerful act of love. Our Lord says, *'He who overcomes, I will make him a pillar in the temple of My God, and he shall go out no more. I will write on him the name of My God and the name of the city of My God, the New Jerusalem, which comes down out of heaven from My God. And I will write on him My new name.'*

They are God's Temple Priests. In Revelation 3:8-11 it says *'I know your works. See, I have set before you an open door, and no one can shut it; for you have a little strength, have kept My word, and have not denied My name. Indeed, I will make those of the synagogue of Satan, who say they are Jews and are not, but lie — indeed I will make them come and worship before your feet, and to know that I have loved you. Because you have kept My command to persevere, I also will keep you from the hour of trial which shall come upon the whole world, to test those who dwell on the earth. Behold, I am coming quickly! Hold fast what you have, that no one may take your crown.'*

They have been persecuted by the unholy trinity and now they are exhausted both physically and spiritually, yet they stand fast. They will soon be sealed with the third Holy Sacrament by our Lord just like their fellow brethren and this takes place in Heaven."

Maria said, "The Marriage Ceremony and Supper is much more involved than one could possibly imagine."

"Very true," replied Mel, "and speaking of involved, the next group also fits that description.

REFINED, ETERNITY-REDEEMED SOULS

They repented after death and received the three Holy Sacraments by those Apostles commissioned by Christ to perform them, here on earth. This is called 'Baptism for the Dead', first commenced by the Apostles of Christ after their Lord's Martyrdom."

Maria asked, "Why are these souls taken from the billions of other souls in eternity, who only during the 1000-Year Kingdom are testified unto?"

Mel's answer, "Three reasons; prayers, grace, and they believed. And by the way, those who live a God-fearing life during the 1000-year Kingdom will be numbered unto the Redeemed, for God wants all souls to be saved.

As to the vast numbers of souls in Eternity and as to where they all came from, Remember Jesus said, 'In my Father's house are many mansions' (large dwelling places)."

CHAPTER TEN:

THE HEALING WATERS AND TREES

ow, Mel said, "I will discuss the 'River of Life', we have information from the book of Revelation and Ezekiel as follows.

In Revelation 22: 1-5 *And he showed me a pure river of water of life, clear as crystal, proceeding from the throne of God and of the Lamb. In the middle of its street, and on either side of the river, was the tree of life, which bore twelve fruits, each tree yielding its fruit every month. The leaves of the tree were for the healing of the nations. And there shall be no more curse, but the throne of God and of the Lamb shall be in it, and His servants shall serve Him. They shall see His face, and His name shall be on their foreheads. There shall be no night there: They need no lamp nor light of the sun, for the Lord God gives them light. And they shall reign forever and ever.*

This pure river of water of life fed the tree of life, which bore twelve fruits, each tree yielding its fruit every month. The leaves of the tree were for the healing of the nations.

As to the names of the twelve fruits, that's a story for another time. As to the leaves, they are necessary for the healing of the nations. How long do you think it will take for all to fully comprehend God's love?

Can you imagine trees and crops giving forth their fruits monthly? No more hunger just like in the beginning, in the Garden of Eden. Even prior to the Rapture the earth produced sufficient food to feed all living upon earth. Imagine what can be accomplished with twelve crops each year. Mankind and all God's creatures shall

| 57

live off the abundance of the land. As to life within the waters, you'll be amazed, again a story for another time when mortality takes on immortality or as I say, eternal life.

CHAPTER ELEVEN:

THE PROPHET EZEKIEL,
IN THE OLD TESTAMENT

The Prophet Ezekiel describes the river of life and how vast it becomes. The following is very interesting should you care to read it, failing which, skip over it like Joe did.

Ezekiel 47

Then he brought me back to the door of the temple; and there was water, flowing from under the threshold of the temple toward the east, for the front of the temple faced east; the water was flowing from under the right side of the temple, south of the altar.

He brought me out by way of the north gate, and led me around on the outside to the outer gateway that faces east; and there was water, running out on the right side.

And when the man went out to the east with the line in his hand, he measured one thousand cubits, and he brought me through the waters;

THE WATER CAME UP TO MY ANKLES.

Again he measured one thousand and brought me through the waters;

THE WATER CAME UP TO MY KNEES.

Again he measured one thousand and brought me through;

THE WATER CAME UP TO MY WAIST.

Again he measured one thousand,

AND IT WAS A RIVER THAT I COULD NOT CROSS; FOR THE WATER WAS TOO DEEP, WATER IN WHICH ONE MUST SWIM, A RIVER THAT COULD NOT BE CROSSED.

He said to me, "Son of man, have you seen this?" Then he brought me and returned me to the bank of the river.

When I returned, there, along the bank of the river, were very many trees on one side and the other.

Then he said to me: "This water flows toward the eastern region, goes down into the valley, and enters the sea. <u>When it reaches the sea, its waters are healed</u>.

<u>And it shall be that every living thing that moves</u>, wherever the rivers go, will live.

There will be a very great multitude of fish, because these waters go there; for they will be healed, and everything will live wherever the river goes.

It shall be that fishermen will stand by it from En Gedi to En Eglaim; they will be places for spreading their nets. Their fish will be of the same kinds as the fish of the Great Sea, exceedingly many.

BUT ITS SWAMPS AND MARSHES WILL NOT BE HEALED; THEY WILL BE GIVEN OVER TO SALT.

Along the bank of the river, on this side and that, will grow all kinds of trees used for food; their leaves will not wither, and their fruit will not fail.

THEY WILL BEAR FRUIT EVERY MONTH, BECAUSE THEIR WATER FLOWS FROM THE SANCTUARY. THEIR FRUIT WILL BE FOR FOOD, <u>AND THEIR LEAVES FOR MEDICINE</u>."

Thus says the Lord God: "These are the borders by which you shall divide the land as an inheritance among the <u>twelve tribes of Israel</u>. Joseph shall have two portions.

You shall inherit it equally with one another; for I raised My hand in an oath to give it to your fathers, and this land shall fall to you as your inheritance.

CHAPTER TWELVE:

BORDERS OF THE NEW JERUSALEM

ow Ezekiel measures the size of the New Jerusalem, it is massive.

Ezekiel 48
Division of the Land
The Gates of the City and Its Name

"These are the exits of the city.

On the __north side__, measuring four thousand five hundred cubits (the gates of the city shall be named after the tribes of Israel), the **THREE GATES** *northward: one gate for Reuben, one gate for Judah, and one gate for Levi;*

on the __east side__, four thousand five hundred cubits, **THREE GATES**: *one gate for Joseph, one gate for Benjamin, and one gate for Dan;*

on the __south side__, measuring four thousand five hundred cubits, **THREE GATES**: *one gate for Simeon, one gate for Issachar, and one gate for Zebulun;*

on the __west side__, four thousand five hundred cubits with their **THREE GATES**: *one gate for Gad, one gate for Asher, and one gate for Naphtali.*

All the way around shall be eighteen thousand cubits;

and the name of the city from that day shall be:

'THE LORD IS THERE'. "

CHAPTER THIRTEEN:

ISRAELITES WHO HEEDED THE OFFER OF SALVATION IN ETERNITY

ow Mel began; "So let's talk about the Israelite Nation."
Tom asked, "What do you mean by the Nation of Israel?"

Mel's answer was, as usual, to the point, "All who still required salvation. Here is wisdom, many souls took to heart the future promise of salvation, concerning the 1000-Years. The following references illustrate this.

Noah, about 2000 BC,

Jesus, the Son of God went to those who died before and during the sin-flood of Noah's time and testified unto them, that salvation would be forthcoming. These souls are brought back to life by God, for the 1000-Year Kingdom, to work out their soul-salvation. Remember those who perished in the sin flood, consisted mostly of the 'bad, evil-seeds.'"

Tom commented, "There is a saying that goes something like this, 'wise learn from the mistakes of others, fools only from their own.'"

"Sadly, true." said Mel, "And now, here's another reference.

Moses, about 1400 BC,

Note, (his bones could not be found on earth by Satan, upon his death)

These are the souls, who were born following the flood of Noah's time, up to the time of Moses and who were led into the Promised Land.

Moses, was on the Mount of Transfiguration[4] with Elijah, both from eternity who were in the presence of God and Jesus when God spoke, as recorded in Luke 9:35 And a voice came out of the cloud, saying, 'This is My Beloved Son... Hear Him!' Also included, were Apostles of Jesus observing.

Moses proclaimed and testified that salvation would be forthcoming, to those who were under his auspices. These souls are brought back to life by God, for the 1000-Year Kingdom, to work out their soul-salvation.

Elijah, about 900 BC,

Note: He never died but ascended to heaven, alive, in a chariot of fire.

Elijah proclaimed and testified that salvation would be forthcoming, to those who were under his auspices. These souls were a continuation from the time of Moses to Elijah and up to the time of Daniel. These souls are brought back to life by God, for the 1000-Year Kingdom, to work out their soul-salvation.

Daniel, about 538 BC,

Daniel was an enigma. He was devoted to his God, and those who followed him were also devoted to his God. From the time of Daniel to the birth of Jesus there were many devoted   and Godly Israelites such as, Shadrach, Meshack and Abednego and their descendants. Daniel's service to the Babylonian and Persian rulers helped to sustain the cohesiveness of the Jews, up to the coming of the Son of God.

Daniel proclaimed and testified that salvation would be forthcoming, to those who were under his auspices. These souls are brought back to life by God, for the 1000-Year Kingdom, to work out their soul-salvation."

Mel turned to Tom saying, "Since you like facts and figures, consider this. The Prophet Daniel (Daniel 9:24) was tutored by the Archangel Gabriel saying, 'Seventy weeks are determined for your people and for your holy city.

The correct interpretation is seventy weeks of years, 70 x 7 = 490 years. With respect to (Daniel 9:24) Daniels prophecy, 70 x 7 = 490, we see that there are 70 blocks of 7 years.

Further, we read in (Daniel 9:27) *Then he shall confirm a cove-nant with many for <u>one week</u>; But in the <u>middle of the week</u>, he shall bring an end to sacrifice and offering. And on the wing of abominations shall be one who makes desolate, even until the consummation, which is determined, is poured out on the desolate."*

Daniel is told that during the 69th week meaning the last week, of the 70 weeks of years. In the middle of this last week being 3½ years, the evil one (Satan) breaks his covenant.

It is noteworthy that Daniel and all Jews consider their Holy City is Jerusalem, although Daniel lived most of his life in Babylon. The Israelites in captivity looked to Daniel for guidance.

Jesus said to forgive your brother 70 x 7 = 490 times, this clari-fies the seventy weeks spoken of by the Archangel Gabriel.

In Revelations, during the 7-Year Great Tribulation there are two 3½ year time periods. See, Daniel is connected to the Book of Revelations concerning a future time, I will leave it at that for now, but to further clarify the above, in the Bible, Daniel (who is told by God the following, concerning those who come back to life.) Daniel 12: 1-2 (excerpt):

AND AT THAT TIME <u>YOUR PEOPLE</u> SHALL BE DELIVERED

Remember Daniel while in eternity was in the midst of <u>his peo-ple</u> and gave testimony to them.

<u>EVERYONE WHO IS FOUND WRITTEN IN THE BOOK.</u>

Israelites, who during the 1000-Years who accept the Holy Sac-raments and remain loyal to God will have their names erased from the Judgment Day book(s) and entered into the Book of Life."

Maria questioned, "Who is to be considered the House of Israel?"

Mel replied, "These are the Israelites in eternity who were testi-fied unto. Again, in the same chapter in the Bible it says:

<u>AND MANY OF THOSE WHO SLEEP IN THE DUST OF THE EARTH SHALL AWAKE.</u>

Most, but not all of the Israelite nation is brought back to life during the 1000-Year Kingdom.

SOME TO EVERLASTING LIFE

Of the Israelite Nation brought back to <u>physical life</u> by God during the 1000-Year Kingdom, they will live outside and next to the walls of the New Jerusalem. They live in peace and God provides all necessities of life for them. They can live for the entire duration of the millennium.

They are the 12 tribes of Israel but unfortunately many gravitate into 'evil-seeds'. Remember 'Of those who sleep…

SOME SHALL AWAKEN TO SHAME

…but they have 1000-Years to make things right.

SOME SHALL AWAKEN TO EVERLASTING CONTEMPT.

These are those referred to as the 'Evil Seeds' who gravitate quickly during the 1000-Years to the areas that are referred to as Gog and His Magog followers. Pure anti-God and evil, they will suffer the consequences, everlasting contempt terminating with, 'Judgment Day'.

See, concerning Daniel, it says: 'But you, go your way till the end; for you shall <u>rest</u>, and will arise to your inheritance at the <u>end of the days</u>.'

So, Daniel is instructed to '<u>rest</u>' until the appointed time."

Maria added; "The Martyrs 'under the altar' were also instructed to '<u>rest</u>' and, using my words…until the appointed time."

"Yes, and next it says, "<u>Arise</u> to <u>your</u> inheritance <u>at the end of the days</u>." The meaning of 'Your inheritance' is that Daniel's and the other select group of names are written into the Book of Life."

Joe asked, "Is Daniel part of the Bride and Wife, and is his name recorded in the "Lambs Book of Life?"

Mel again smiled saying, "Why don't you ask the person whose plate you took the food from, when you get back to the Marriage Feast."

Joe replied, "That was Daniel, but how can he be "Past, Present and Future?""

Mel chuckled saying, "I just love cryptic timeline shifting." Joe did not fall for this line a third time, and simply smiled.

"God's plan of salvation is so complicated yet marvelous," Maria sighed. These exact same words gently echoed in the back of her mind, from times past.

She then enquired, "What about the Israelites who lived from Jesus time unto the present time?"

Mel simply replied, "Some, during these years accepted the testimony of the Apostles of Christ, others rejected, while others simply, never heard of God's plan of salvation."

CHAPTER FOURTEEN:

AN ARMY OF ISRAELITE SKELETONS, BROUGHT BACK TO LIFE

" Now we come to a very strange group of people, a nation." Mel stated. "<u>There will arise another nation, an Army that comes up out of the ground and comes back to life, also in one day</u>.

Mel then said, "They form part of the Citizens of the 1000 Year Kingdom and are given a second chance for salvation."

We read in, Revelation 3:18, *'I counsel you to buy from Me gold refined in the fire, that you may be rich; and white garments, that you may be clothed, that the shame of your nakedness may not be revealed; and anoint your eyes with eye salve, that you may see.'*

Thousands of years ago, as recorded in the Bible, God spoke to His Prophet Ezekiel. In Ezekiel 36:24 it says *For I will take you from among the nations, gather you out of all countries, and bring you into your own land.*

God will gather all Israelites together into a land of their own.

25 **<u>Then I will sprinkle clean water on you</u>, and <u>you shall be clean</u>; **<u>I will cleanse you from all your filthiness</u> and <u>from all your idols.</u>*
   *This is the Holy Baptism of Water.
   **This is the Holy Communion.
31 *Then you will remember your evil ways and your deeds that were not good; and you will loathe yourselves in your own sight, for your iniquities and your abominations.*

However, their past is not removed from their thoughts, they must overcome, be and remain loyal to their God.

33 *Thus says the Lord God: "On the day that I cleanse you from all your iniquities, I will also enable you to dwell in the cities, and the ruins shall be rebuilt.*

34 *The desolate land shall be tilled instead of lying desolate in the sight of all who pass by.*

35 *So they will say, 'This land that was desolate has become like the garden of Eden; and the wasted, desolate, and ruined cities are now fortified and inhabited.'*

They will dwell in cities and rebuild the ruins, once again farm the land and it will become like the garden of Eden that was 'Paradise on Earth'."

People loyal to God will not kill animals for food, they will live off the land. It is written in Isaiah 66:3 that during this time if one were to kill a bull it would be as bad as if they killed a man. Also, if one kills a lamb it's as grievous as **if they killed a dog**. This shows unto all how elevated dogs are in the eyes of God, which by the way is His name spelled backwards. Also note, every language in past times had the word 'DOG' and nobody knows how this came into being but I can guess you three do now. One final tidbit of information, only during the last century did people begin once again naming their pets as Adam did in the Garden of Eden. Once named, they are elevated to family members.

This demonstrates that during this time period known as the 1000-Year Kingdom when God's Holy City, the New Jerusalem is upon earth, dogs next to humans are very special. People even today have dreams whereby their pets are shown waiting for them with joyful expectations, for there will be no broken hearts in Heaven. The New Jerusalem embodies the former Garden of Eden, the difference this time is that God, His Son & Wife and many more also live there.

36 Then the nations which are left <u>all around you</u> shall know that I, the Lord, have rebuilt the ruined places and planted what was desolate. I, the Lord, have spoken it, and I will do it.'

Surrounding God's People will be others who witness God's handiwork; however, their hearts once again revert back to the old ways, 'Evil'

Their old ways include killings of men and animals, for 'evil grows'.

38 Like a flock offered as holy sacrifices, like the flock at Jerusalem on its feast days, so shall the ruined cities be filled with flocks of men. Then they shall know that I am the Lord.

The new cities will have congregations who worship God.

Technology will not evolve; however, swords, spears, bows and arrows, you could say simple weapons will be made by the evil Gog and his Magog nations."

Tom asked, "Those outside the walls, do they ever come inside?"

Mel answered, "Yes, those who accept the offer of salvation consisting of the 3 Holy Sacraments and keep their garments pure do, during the feast of the tabernacles that occurs once each year. However, most migrate further and further away. Their fate sealed.

Maria commented, "Oh yes, Gog and Magog, the anti-God along with his anti-God nations and people."

Mel continued, "God will call the Nation of Israel out of the ground. This has been a religious conundrum for millennia, however, now it will be explained.

In the Bible, in Ezekiel 37 we can now read how God makes it happen, and Joe, this is important so don't skip over it.

1 The hand of the Lord came upon me and brought me out in the Spirit of the Lord, <u>and set me down in the midst of the valley; and it was full of bones.</u>

2 Then He caused me to pass by them all around, and behold, there were very many in the open valley; and indeed they were very dry.

3 And He said to me, "Son of man, can these bones live?" So I answered, "O Lord God, You know."

4 Again He said to me, "Prophesy to these bones, and say to them, 'O dry bones, hear the word of the Lord!

5 Thus says the Lord God to these bones: "Surely I will cause breath to enter into you, and you shall live.

6 I will put sinews on you and bring flesh upon you, cover you with skin and put breath in you; and you shall live. Then you shall know that I am the Lord.""

7 So I prophesied as I was commanded; and as I prophesied, there was a noise, and suddenly a rattling; and the bones came together, bone to bone.

8 Indeed, as I looked, the sinews and the flesh came upon them, and the skin covered them over; but there was no breath in them.

9 Also He said to me, "Prophesy to the breath, prophesy, son of man, and say to the breath, 'Thus says the Lord God: "Come from the four winds, O breath, and breathe on these slain, that they may live."

10 So I prophesied as He commanded me, and breath came into them, and they lived, and stood upon their feet, an exceedingly great army.

11 Then He said to me, "Son of man, these bones are the whole house of Israel. They indeed say, 'Our bones are dry, our hope is lost, and we ourselves are cut off!'

12 Therefore prophesy and say to them, Thus says the Lord God: 'Behold, O My people, I will open your graves and cause you to come up from your graves, and bring you into the land of Israel.'"

Mel said to Joe, "Ok let's pause and summarize what was just read.

The dead nation of Israel is brought back to mortal life and placed on earth, by God.

They will live outside of the New Jerusalem in 12 tribes, each tribe having a designated sector and will be living off the land.

During the once a year 'Feast of the Tabernacles' those who have matured in faith are allowed entry into the New Jerusalem (but not into the Temple)to bring their offerings. Their offerings are brought on horses having bells that create a wonderful sound of thanksgiving.

Over time, the good remain connected to the New Jerusalem and I might add, the protection of God. The bad, overtime, migrate outwards to the coastal areas, and the anti-God.

All people who remain faithful to their God will have their names removed from the Judgment Day and entered into the Book of Life.

They may live outside the New Jerusalem; however, they are protected from the evil growing around them. And as I previously said, some will be allowed into the New Jerusalem. However, only the Royal Kings will be allowed to bring their offerings into the Temple of God."

Maria commented, "It seems extremely complicated to me. Are you saying that certain Israelites received salvation in eternity while others must attain it in human form?" Mel only smiled.

ONE KINGDOM, ONE KING

Without missing a beat, Mel continued reading then summarizing Ezekiel 37: 15 – 22.

15 Again the word of the Lord came to me, saying,

16 "As for you, son of man, take a stick for yourself and write on it:

'For Judah and for the children of Israel, his companions.'

Then take another stick and write on it,

'For Joseph, the stick of Ephraim, and for all the house of Israel, his companions.'

17 Then join them one to another for yourself into one stick, and they will become one in your hand.

18 "And when the children of your people speak to you, saying, 'Will you not show us what you mean by these?'

19 say to them, 'Thus says the Lord God: "Surely I will take the stick of Joseph, which is in the hand of Ephraim, and the tribes of Israel, his companions; and I will join them with it, with the stick of Judah, and make them one stick, and they will be one in My hand."'

20 And the sticks on which you write will be in your hand before their eyes.

*21 "Then say to them, '**Thus says the Lord God: "Surely I will take the children of Israel from among the nations, wherever they have gone, and will gather them from every side and bring them into their own land;***

22 and I will make them one nation in the land, <u>on the mountains of Israel;</u> and one king shall be king over them all; they shall no longer be two nations, nor shall they ever be divided into two kingdoms again.

The New Jerusalem that comes down from Heaven is about 1400 miles square.

There are over 20 mountain ranges within the boundaries of the New Jerusalem.

The New Jerusalem having God's Holy Mountain in its center is massive and extends upwards 1400 miles and is tethered to Heaven directly above it. The New Jerusalem is not a cube, more like a pyramid having its length, width, and height at about 1400 miles.

Within the walls of the New Jerusalem there are over 1 billion acres of land and one acre of farmland can support one person, this equals 1 billion people.

Now consider, within the New Jerusalem the trees will give their harvest every month, the same applies to all the farmer's crops. You can clearly see that within the walls of the New Jerusalem seemingly tens of billions of people could live in peace, live off the land, truly a new nation of God loving humans.

They live in the Garden yes, the actual Garden that was originally placed by God <u>in the east of Eden</u> for Adam and Eve, has once again been placed upon earth. Now you know the massive size of Eden that was created for Adam and Eve along with all the animal kingdom, for God once said to Job, "Everything under Heaven is Mine." This has vastly, far greater implications, that I will elaborate on later. What is referred to as the "Garden of Eden" was actually only the easterly portion of Eden, the Garden.

Now, if you have the faith to comprehend, God's animal kingdom does not have nor need a 'soul', however they do have a life force, their 'spirit'. During the 1000-Year Kingdom the full complement of God's creation will also rise to the absolute delight of humans. In past times, many millions have had the honor of caring for some of His creation.

Maria asked; Will those who were kind unto God's creation have a special place in God's heart? Mel's eyes sparkled or teared, Maria could not tell for sure, but his actions answered her. Mel continued reading.

23 They shall not defile themselves anymore with their idols, nor with their detestable things, nor with any of their transgressions; but I will deliver them from all their dwelling places in which they have sinned, <u>and will cleanse them</u>. Then they shall be My people, and I will be their God.

*24 **<u>David My servant shall be king over them</u>**, and they shall all have one shepherd; they shall also walk in My judgments and observe My statutes and do them.*

The Psalmist David will be their king over those God brought up from their graves, the Nation of Israel, who dwell in the 12 Tribes surrounding the Walls of the New Jerusalem.

CHAPTER FIFTEEN:

WHO LIVES IN OR AROUND THE NEW JERUSALEM?

o, the 1000-year time-period begins, peace for some but no peace for most.

Mel now began talking about those who dwell within or live outside, surrounding the New Jerusalem as follows.

1. Royal Kings (Spiritual Beings) live inside.
2. Royal Priests (Spiritual Beings) live inside.
3. Temple Priests (Spiritual Beings) live inside.
4. Testifier Priests (Spiritual Beings) live inside.
5. Redeemed from eternity (Spiritual Beings) live inside.
6. Israelite Army of the Dead (Physical Bodies) live outside
7. Saved Nations (bad and good) (Physical Bodies) live outside

"The Children of God dwell within this glorious walled city; some remain within God's Temple while others in their various capacities proclaim God's Will like preachers of the past, but no longer confined to buildings, to those living outside the walls." Joe was amazed yet again as he saw how there were children playing with their pets in the new kingdom. Somehow, someway love survives and is not restricted only to humans.

Mel, commented, "God sees the little sparrow fall, if you believe, it will happen".

Maria sighed, "God's plan is all about love."

"Yes," replied Mel, "and while in human form one cannot fathom the scope of God's love. Only now is it beginning to sink in, and you haven't even scratched the surface yet."

Maria, quivering, said, "I'm feeling scared for some reason."

Mel reassured her saying, "Actually Maria you're experiencing 'awe' and that's a good thing." Mel went a little further saying "Remember this parable. A wise man once said to a young child; 'are you wise?' 'No' replied the lad and the wise man smiled saying that that was the beginning of wisdom.' Now look back, what do you also see?"

All three replied that they saw the beloved city of God, the New Jerusalem.

Joe commented that it was huge, with God's Holy Mountain in its center. Mel elevated them upwards (really upwards) for a better view.

Tom broke the awed silence of the three, saying, "Now I get it! In the past when I read that it was 1400 miles square and its height was the same, I couldn't fathom how something square could land upon the earth. The Holy City seems to gently rest upon the earth's surface yet its walls remain at a constant height almost as if it's bending to the curvature of the earth."

Joe, nodding, added, "Not only does it rest on the earth's surface, it actually follows the contours of the land including the mountains and valleys. How this can be, escapes me. One thing is for sure: God's Holy Mountain is massive. It has many plateaus until its highest point in the center is tethered to Heaven high above it."

Mel advanced the timeline slightly and they now saw God's children inside the walls along with many multitudes. They watched and saw the setting up of the 12 tribes of Israel encompassing outside the walls. Surrounding them were the saved, consisting of the bad and good. Both groups will have those who develop over time into camps, villages and cities. Many will migrate further and further away to the remote portions of the rejoined land mass and the coastal areas. They devolve into the anti-God having Gog as their leader and his Magog nations who follow him.

CHAPTER SIXTEEN:

THE TEMPLE,
THE LORD'S DWELLING PLACE

Mel continued, "Now, God again speaks to Ezekiel as recorded in Ezekiel 43:1-6. After we read these few verses I will explain them.

Ezekiel 43
1 Afterward he brought me to the gate, the gate that faces toward the east. 2 And behold, the glory of the God of Israel came from the way of the east. His voice was like the sound of many waters; and the earth shone with His glory. 3 It was like the appearance of the vision which I saw—like the vision which I saw when I came to destroy the city. The visions were like the vision which I saw by the River Chebar; and I fell on my face. 4 And the glory of the Lord came into the temple by way of the gate which faces toward the east. 5 The Spirit lifted me up and brought me into the inner court; and behold, the glory of the Lord filled the temple.

6 Then I heard Him speaking to me from the temple, while a man stood beside me. 7 And He said to me, <u>"Son of man, this is the place of My throne and the place of the soles of My feet, where I will dwell in the midst of the children of Israel forever.</u>

This is the law of the temple:
The whole area surrounding the mountaintop is most holy.
Behold, this is the law of the temple.

"The entire area within the New Jerusalem is most holy, however, outside of it, evil grows. The earth, during the 1000-Year time-period, undergoes a most unique transformation. The waters, formerly blood, now receive the healing waters from God. The continents have by this time recombined into one large land mass surrounded entirely by the great sea. The New Jerusalem with God's Holy Mountain is at its center along with all the holy mountains within its walls."

CHAPTER SEVENTEEN:

SAVED NATIONS SURROUND
THE 12 TRIBES OF ISRAEL

It is interesting to note that the 12 Tribes of Israel do not live within the New Jerusalem, rather they live outside its four walls on its north, south, east, and west sides. Also, the saved nations live on the outskirts of the 12 Tribes of Israel, like concentric squares. Also, on a sad-note, those who are indifferent to God migrated to the outer limits, as far away from God as possible.

The recombined continents have now formed one large land mass as the Apostle John saw in Revelations 21:1 Now I saw a new heaven and a new earth, for the first heaven and the first earth had passed away.

Mel said, "Now we will discuss the 'saved nations' who came from the Time of God's 2 Ambassadors. Those of the nations saved were the worthy guests in Marriage Feast as recorded in Revelation 21:24-27.

And the nations of those who are saved shall walk in its light, and the kings of the earth bring their glory and honor into it. Its gates shall not be shut at all by day (there shall be no night there). And they shall bring the glory and the honor of the nations into it. But there shall by no means enter it anything that defiles, or causes an abomination or a lie, but only those who are written in the **Lamb's Book of Life.**

Mel said, "Only those who are written in **the Lamb's Book of Life** can enter God's Holy City. This City of God does not require the light of the sun as the Glory of God illumines it.

CHAPTER EIGHTEEN:

THE NATIONS WORSHIP THE KING

Mel continued, now comes a blessing or curse.

16 And it shall come to pass that everyone who is left of all the nations which came against Jerusalem shall <u>go up from year to year to worship the King, the Lord of hosts, and to keep the Feast of Tabernacles.</u>

*17 And it shall be that whichever of the families of the earth <u>do not come up to Jerusalem to worship the King, the Lord of hosts,</u> on **them there will be no rain.***

18 If the family of Egypt will not come up and enter in, they shall have no rain; they shall receive the plague with which the Lord strikes the nations who do not come up to keep the Feast of Tabernacles.

19 This shall be the punishment of Egypt and the punishment of all the nations that do not come up to keep the Feast of Tabernacles.

Mel told them that the above was most unique because those who do not obey God's commands and that do not come up to keep the Feast of Tabernacles will suffer once again plagues but never again the plague of the blood-virus, this was a one-time occurrence.

As recorded in Zechariah 14: 16-21 in that day '**HOLINESS TO THE LORD**'. *<u>shall be engraved on the bells of the horses. The pots in the Lord's house shall be like the bowls before the altar. 21 Yes, every pot in Jerusalem and Judah shall be holiness to the Lord of hosts. Every-</u>*

one who sacrifices shall come and take them and cook in them. In that day there shall no longer be a Canaanite in the house of the Lord of hosts

Mel said, "The Prophet Isaiah has something to add to this concerning the future house of God in Isaiah 2:4 The Future House of God The word that Isaiah the son of Amoz saw concerning Judah and Jerusalem."

Now it shall come to pass in the latter days that <u>the mountain of the Lord's house shall be established</u> <u>on the top of the mountains</u>, and shall be exalted above the hills and all nations shall flow to it. Many people shall come and say, "Come, and let us go up to the mountain of the Lord, to the house of the God of Jacob. He will teach us His ways, and we shall walk in His paths. For out of Zion shall go forth the law, and the word of the Lord from Jerusalem. He shall judge between the nations, and rebuke many people.

Joe commented, "Seems like there is a mountain upon mountains, the New Jerusalem rests upon the tops of the mountains, this sentence is very clever, for it says… the New Jerusalem rests upon the TOPS of the MOUNTAINS." This again shows the immense size of it.

"True." replied Mel, "They shall beat their swords into plowshares, and their spears into pruning hooks. Nation shall not lift up sword against nation, neither shall they learn war anymore.

And here is another passage which is loaded with information."

Isaiah 65:20-25 says,

"There shall be no more thence an infant of days, nor an old man that hath not filled his days: <u>for the child shall die a hundred years old;</u> but the sinner being a hundred years old shall be accursed.

And they shall build houses, and inhabit them; and they shall plant vineyards, and eat the fruit of them.

<u>They shall not build, and another inhabit; they shall not plant, and another eat</u>: for as the days of a tree are the days of my people, and mine elect shall long enjoy the work of their hands.

They shall not labour in vain, nor bring forth for trouble; for they are the seed of the blessed of the LORD, and their offspring with them.

And it shall come to pass, that before they call, I will answer; and while they are yet speaking, I will hear.

The wolf and the lamb shall feed together, and the lion shall eat straw like the bullock: and dust shall be the serpent's meat. They shall not hurt nor destroy in all my holy mountain, saith the LORD."

Maria added that in the beginning from Adam to Noah given in Genesis 5 and 9:29, they have extremely long-life spans over 900 years and now this longevity was once again brought back.

Mel said, "Bear in mind though these people and their descendants will be capable of both sin and death in the millennial kingdom, even though Satan will be in chains and unable to influence them, evil flourishes.

It is of paramount importance that you comprehend the last sentence as follows.

They shall not hurt nor destroy in all my holy mountain, saith the LORD.

See, all life is sacred to God, His people will never again kill to survive. Now we also read that following description of the New Heaven:

Ezekiel 37:25-26 says, "And they shall dwell in the land that I have given unto Jacob my servant, wherein your fathers have dwelt; and they shall dwell therein, even they, and their children, and their children's children for ever: and my servant David shall be their prince forever. Moreover, I will make a covenant of peace with them; it shall be an everlasting covenant with them: and I will place them, and multiply them, and will set my sanctuary in the midst of them for evermore."

CHAPTER NINETEEN:

ISRAEL WILL BE A KINGDOM OF PRIESTS

In Zechariah 8:20-23 And in Exodus19:5-6 it describes in great detail some of the events during the 1000-year Kingdom.

"Thus saith the LORD of hosts; It shall yet come to pass, that there shall come people, and the inhabitants of many cities: And the inhabitants of one city shall go to another, saying, Let us go speedily to pray before the LORD, and to seek the LORD of hosts: I will go also. Yea, many people and strong nations shall come to seek the LORD of hosts in Jerusalem, and to pray before the LORD. Thus saith the LORD of hosts; In those days it shall come to pass, that ten men shall take hold out of all languages of the nations, even shall take hold of the skirt of him that is a Jew, saying, we will go with you: for we have heard that God is with you" (Zechariah 8:20-23).

"Now therefore, <u>if ye will obey my voice indeed,</u> and <u>keep my covenant,</u> then ye shall be a peculiar treasure unto me above all people: for all the earth is mine: <u>And ye shall be unto me a kingdom of priests, and a holy nation.</u> These are the words which thou shalt speak unto the children of Israel" (Exodus 19:5-6)."

Mel added, "To be clear, it says, '<u>if</u> ye will obey my voice indeed, and keep my covenant.' We know that as sand of the sea, they don't."

CHAPTER TWENTY:

EVIL-SEEDS IN THE KINGS HALL

"**M**any are called but few are chosen."

Even though the words were directed to Satan, all in attendance heard this sentence. This caused many of the evil-seeds to involuntary quiver while future evil-seeds were oblivious to their nature and would only find out later what truly lived within their souls.

Joe murmured, "See that fellow over there? His head has been bowed all this time. I wonder why?"

Mel smiled saying, "So you caught that, did you?"

Tom chimed in, "Who is he?"

Mel sighed, "We will discuss Gog later." And left it at that.

Maria silently thought that it was sad that a person's hidden nature and inclinations eventually does them in. They are the evil-seeds and perhaps don't even know it.

As if sensing where her thoughts had gone, Mel said, "The 'evil-seeds' are necessary for the 'saved nations' to prove to God that they are deserving of His Grace and Mercy. For example, Job had to be tested and likewise everyone must be tested sooner or later. God gives unto human's free will. They are not commanded to be faithful and loyal unto Him. Each soul must choose for themselves, their destiny."

Mel went on saying the "saved nations" are gathered and brought to the 'Marriage Feast' within the 'Kings Hall' and this takes place prior to Armageddon.

Maria added, "So even at this late stage with less than 220 days left until Armageddon, God still offered salvation to humans."

Tom pointed to vast numbers of people all dressed in white garments, commenting, "Truly a most awesome and remarkable sight". They saw how the people did not walk into the hall rather they were materializing and simultaneously being seated in some type of pre-arranged arrangement."

Joe commented that Heaven certainly has order to it and Maria quipped, "Ya think?"

Continuing Joe said, "The Marriage Feast in the Kings Hall is enormous. See the tables and chairs all arranged in rows upon rows arranged in a 3-dimentional pattern."

Tom said, that enormous would be putting it mildly, and directed a question to Mel, "When does the feast actually commence?"

Mel replied, "When God's two Witnesses are brought back to life and are transported up from the earth to God in Heaven. This is the trigger. During these last 220 days prior to Armageddon, the 'Saved' are ushered in and seated, for they are still in their human bodies. The dimension of time no longer exists, and to those seated, it only seems like minutes until the feast begins. Upon Satan being cast out of the Kings Hall, Armageddon commences and in what seems like a flash of a great sword, the Marriage Feast in the Kings Hall begins, and what a spectacular sight it is."

Maria asked, "What are we doing during this time?"

"Watching." replied Mel.

Tom then asked, "Watching what?"

Maria answered, "Why, the Armageddon battle of course."

Mel added, "Yes, correct. All in the great hall view the battle from their vantage point. From its start to finish it seems to take mere seconds for earth-time no longer applies. They experience Christ on a White Horse as recorded in Revelation 19: 11-16. Tom please read this.

Now I saw heaven opened, and behold, a white horse. And He who sat on him was called Faithful and True, and in righteousness He judges and makes war. 12 His eyes were like a flame of fire, and on His head were many crowns. He had a name written that no one knew except

Himself. 13 He was clothed with a robe dipped in blood, and His name is called The Word of God. 14 And the armies in heaven, clothed in fine linen, white and clean, followed Him on white horses. 15 <u>Now out of His mouth goes a sharp sword,</u> that with it He should strike the nations. And He Himself will rule them with a rod of iron. He Himself treads the winepress of the fierceness and wrath of Almighty God. 16 And He has on His robe and on His thigh a name written".

KING OF KINGS AND LORD OF LORDS.

Mel ended his thought saying, "That's enough information for now, let's go to the 1000-Year Kingdom and see all the happenings.

Tom added that "Right up to the last 15 months when Satan is loose with his 3-demons, and the gathering of the massive satanic armies and the last great battle, and Judgment Day and then the New Heaven and Earth—"

"Whoa, that's a lot of 'ands'!" interjected Joe.

Maria rolled her eyes that special way, seeing Joe's expression who was beside himself in fear of losing that sumptuous meal he had briefly sampled and was drooling over.

Joe protested, "You mean we gotta wait a thousand years before we eat?" he remonstrated.

Mel countered, saying, "Joe how can you still think of your stomach at a time like this?"

Easy for you to say!" he replied. "Does this look like a 'happy face' to you?"

Before Joe's stomach could do anymore grumbling, Mel took them outside the Marriage hall and using one of his signature waves created another time-line-shift, taking them into the lands surrounding it.

"What a change in the scenery!" Maria commented. "So this is what the Garden of Eden must have looked like. Green pastures, fruit trees, and over there it looks like wheat fields, cornfields, and as far as the eye can see there's edible food!"

Joe, now with tears in his eyes, sighed, "Look!" and pointed to vast numbers of animals. "I know some of them."

"Me too." said both Tom and Maria.

Mel smiled gently at them, saying, "Why are you surprised? For it says in Revelation 5:13 *And every creature which is in heaven and on the earth and under the earth and such as are in the sea, and all that are in them, I heard saying: "Blessing and honor and glory and power be to Him who sits on the throne, And to the Lamb, forever and ever!" Also, in Job 41:11 we read…God says, "Everything under heaven is Mine."*

Maria, now startled, whispered, "They're actually speaking somehow just as in the Garden of Eden when Adam named all the animals, for they were family to him. This may be the reason why pets are so important to us."

Tom added, "Only in more recent times humans once again began naming their pets, who again had the status of being family to us."

Mel added, to their amazement, that the way the animals could communicate, included telepathy, as in past times.

"Astonishing." Tom bending down to pet an old friend from his and Joe's childhood. The dog wagged her tail as Tom let her lick his face, and again to his amazement, she communicated with them that she would be eagerly waiting for their return.

Joe perplexed said, "I can't decide did she speak or use telepathy, Mel whispered, "What's the difference Joe, it is what it is" and then all three thought the same thought, they do the same thing.

CHAPTER TWENTY-ONE:

THE 1000-YEARS BEGIN...
NO-PEACE FOR MOST

el beckoned for the three to be silent and pay attention. "Now in the Bible it does not say, 'The 1000-years of peace' the word 'peace' is not mentioned. To those living within and those living immediately surrounding the New Jerusalem there will be peace. To those who migrate to the far lands of Gog and His Magog Nations... no-peace.

Satan, now captured, as recorded in Revelation 20: 1-3 *'Then I saw an angel coming down from heaven, having the key to the bottomless pit and a great chain in his hand. He laid hold of the dragon, that serpent of old, who is the Devil and Satan, and bound him for a thousand years; and he cast him into the bottomless pit, and shut him up, and set a seal on him, so that he should deceive the nations no more till the thousand years were finished. But after these things he must be released for a little while.'*

We can see from this that Satan, by whatever name one may refer to him, is bound for the duration of the 1000-year Kingdom. This allows all people to be able to work out their soul salvation without satanic interference; however, evil grows. At the end, Satan is released from the "pit" for a little while along with his 3-demons, for about 15 months. In Isaiah 2 (NKJV), concerning the Future House of God, it is written:

2
Now it shall come to pass in the latter days
That the mountain of the Lord's house
Shall be established on the top of the mountains,
And shall be exalted above the hills;
And all nations shall flow to it.

Mel smiled saying, this next verse is magnificent.

3
Many people shall come and say,
"Come, and let us go up to the mountain of the Lord,
To the house of the God of Jacob;
He will teach us His ways,
And we shall walk in His paths."
For out of Zion shall go forth the law,
And the word of the Lord from Jerusalem.

4
He shall judge between the nations,
And rebuke many people;
They shall beat their swords into plowshares,
And their spears into pruning hooks;
Nation shall not lift up sword against nation,
Neither shall they learn war anymore.

a. THE GROUPS
Now those living upon the earth, originate from the following groups of people.

<u>First</u>
Those still in their human bodies who came from the 'Kings Marriage Hall' after the 'Marriage feast' of His Son, and all wearing their Marriage garments.

<u>Second</u>
Their descendants who during the 1000-Year Kingdom either listened and accepted the testimony of salvation offered to them, re-

ceived garments of salvation, and kept them pure or drifted away to become the anti-God nations of Gog and his Magog nations.

Third
The Israelite army nation raised up from their graves, they too are from the eternal realms.

Joe asked, "How many people would then inhabit the earth?"

Mel smiled, "Let's just say that 100 billion people could easily fit into the recombined land masses.

Tom added, "The landmass of the recombined earth then would be able to easily support vastly greater numbers, and harvests would be monthly."

Mel finished the conversation by saying, "The anti-God will number as the sand of the sea, God once said to Satan, '*this earth was made for many but Heaven for only a few*'. And another thing, the trees bear their harvests monthly, within the New Jerusalem, outside that's another story. Remember, the disobedient will get no rain, then no harvests in certain areas resulting in continuous raiding of settlements and cities."

"From these groups some have Godly garments and some will get them, however, all must keep their garments pure. If they succeed, their names are removed from the Judgement Day books and subsequently entered into the Book of Life. This is a big 'if'."

"All souls exempted from Judgement Day wear Garments of Salvation and will do so eternally for Satan, his demons and evil, exist no more. This is the way God intended Adam to develop in the beginning."

"During the 1000-Year Kingdom all souls are testified unto, during this time, these souls either are drawn to the light or shun and reject it, becoming or joining the 'evil-seeds' who migrate to the far areas and once again become the anti-God."

"Those drawn to the light accept the testimony given unto them by the Priests of God along with their helpers."

"I have already described the functionality of the Bride, now the Wife of the Son of God. Next, I will discuss their roles, beginning with the firstlings, the Royal Kings and the Royal Priests during the 1000-Year Kingdom."

"The Son of God, prior to the Rapture, said of both groups, *'Well done, thou good and faithful servant; you were faithful over a few things, I will make you ruler over many things. Enter into the joy of your lord.'* "

"Great events now take place and that is why it takes 10 centuries to fulfill. With rejoicing, now we will read again about those special "Children of God", the Royal Kings. They will 'rule with a rod of iron' during the 1000-Year Kingdom. One may ask the question as to why they will have to 'rule with a rod of iron' as this seems so heavy-handed. This control will be necessary because even though there is peace, the nature of people will still be either good or bad and speaking of bad, the evil-seeds will once again germinate into weeds." Joe added that you can't be kind to weeds.

"The Bible says of them in Revelation 15:22

Jesus Testifies to the Churches

12 *"And behold, I am coming quickly, and My reward is with Me, to give to every one according to his work.*

13 *I am the Alpha and the Omega, the Beginning and the End, the First and the Last."*

14 *Blessed are those who do His commandments,*
i. *that they may have the right to the tree of life, and*
ii. *may enter through the gates into the city.*

15 *But outside*
iii. *are dogs and*
iv. *sorcerers and*
v. *sexually immoral and*
vi. *murderers and*
vii. *idolaters,*
viii. *whoever loves and practices a lie.*

"So, if someone says, why they will have to 'rule with a rod of iron' as this seems so heavy-handed, you now have the answer…evil is alive and well."

b. RULE WITH A ROD OF IRON

Mel continued to speak to them, saying, "Out of His mouth went a sword, not of metal but rather of power. And He Himself will rule them with a rod of iron, during the 1000-Year Kingdom that soon follows. As a side note the Bride will also rule with a rod of iron as we saw in Revelation 2:27 because of the evil-seeds, you knew that, right?" They all looked at each other and nodded.

Mel continued, "They will oversee the testimony unto billions of souls and rule with the rod of iron as recorded in Revelation 12:5. *She bore a male Child who was to rule all nations with a rod of iron.* It takes this power to control the 'evil-seeds', these anti-God evil beings. These evil seeds are growing in vast numbers and must be kept in check during the 1000-Year Kingdom."

"The Royal Kings and Royal Priests will continue to offer salvation to all during this time prior to Judgment Day."

"Priests of Christ, we can read of them in, Revelation 6:10-11 *'they were crying with a loud voice, saying, "How long, O Lord until You judge and avenge our blood on those who dwell on the earth?'* They are anxious to go forth as mighty testifiers of their Lord. They were told by Jesus to be patient for a little while until their fellow brethren were killed during the Great Tribulation time. This is a very large group who will be testifying to a vast number of souls giving them the opportunity for salvation. They will prepare those desiring salvation into groups who are waiting for the Royal Kings and Royal Priests and perhaps others."

"The next group, who are from the Great Tribulation that followed the Rapture, will serve God in his Temple. At this time, the tabernacle of God is with men, and He will dwell with them, and they shall be His people."

Maria commented, "And we are part of this group who were Martyred."

"Correct." Mel replied, "Albeit you three were very young when you received the Three Holy Sacraments. You are unique and were the last three Martyrs of Christ bearing the mark of God and of His Son, and that's why you're here with me. I know you have many questions, and all will be answered in due-time. The Apostle John in Revelation 20: 4-6 says, 'and I saw thrones, and they sat on them, and judgment was committed to them'. These are the Royal Kings and Royal Priests."

"Next it reads, 'Then I saw the souls of those who had been beheaded for their witness to Jesus and for the word of God, who had not worshiped the beast or his image, and had not received his mark on their foreheads or on their hands. And they lived and reigned with Christ for a thousand years.'"

"These are the Martyr Priests of Christ who remained faithful to their God and Jesus, during the Great Tribulation. Their reward is, 'Blessed and holy is he who has part in the first resurrection. Over such the second death has no power.'"

"Look carefully, <u>it says of them that the second death has no power.</u> They have part in the first resurrection and function during the 1000-Year Kingdom so their names were not in the Judgment Day Books nor the Book of Life, they were in the Lamb's Book of Life. Remember the 3 books?"

"In Revelation 7:9-17 They are before the throne of God and will serve Him day and night in His temple. Once again, I'm going to paraphrase as it's a long Bible passage. We read that the number is so great they could not be counted. They came from all of the nations, tribes, peoples, and tongues, standing before the throne and before the Lamb, clothed with white robes, with palm branches in their hands, and crying out with a loud voice, saying,

'Salvation belongs to our God who sits on the throne, and to the Lamb!'

'Then one of the elders asked me "Who are these arrayed in white robes, and where did they come from?" So he said to me, "These are the ones who come out of the great tribulation, and washed their robes and made them white in the blood of the Lamb. Therefore, they are before the throne of God, and serve Him day and night in His temple. And God will wipe away every tear from their eyes.'"

Mel continued, "They did not cry out for God to avenge them because they are different in nature. They have palm branches in their hands, they are reconciled meaning they don't seek payback like the first group does and so become the Temple Priests in God's Temple. Remember I said everyone has a function and this is theirs."

Mel continued, "Now, during the 1000-Year Kingdom, there shall be no more (natural) death, nor sorrow, nor crying. There shall be no more pain, for the former things have passed away.' I will give of the fountain of the water of life freely to him who thirsts. Bear in mind, those who drift further and further away must suffer the lack of rainfall, plagues, murder and other calamities."

"One might ask the question could evil souls during these days unworthily partake of the sacraments. The answer, absolutely not, a soul's true nature now becomes fully evident. For clarity you might say an evil soul's color is red, while a repentant soul's color, is white. Their actions justify their end. They are judged and judgement means that they are no more. People during these days, even though they have received their garments of salvation, still can backslide. Remember the 'evil-seeds' will not avail themselves of this extra time of grace, also the descendants of the evil seeds have not received any garments of salvation and must either desire them or not. Sadly, as the 'sand of the sea', they do not."

"Now you see how your Father, God, never gives up on souls. People live in total peace, plenty of food and drink, there is no pecking order, you work you get. People have happy surroundings and even the vicious animals including snakes are docile unto people, they actually play together. Most will live to the conclusion of 1000-Years. Can you image that? The question arises why so many again turn to Satan and his evil ways?" Mel, frustratingly said, "Remember God offers, not mandates, salvation."

c. ROYAL KINGS & ROYAL PRIESTS OF GOD

Mel continued, "As the anti-God grow in massive numbers and boldness, they advance from time to time towards those living in peace surrounding the New Jerusalem whose numbers are in the tens of millions and more. Their goal is to rape, plunder, kill, and loot them of their possessions. Unfortunately for them, they encounter superhuman obstacles, namely the Royal Kings and Royal Priests of God."

"The Royal Kings and Priests, with their immensely powerful "rods of iron" which is a metaphor for energy weapons that knock evil to the ground to, say the least, constantly work to keep the anti-God at bay from the good who are maturing into a Godly state. The power emanating from these "rods of iron" serves as a constant reminder to all witnessing that all power and authority comes from God."

"The Royal Kings and Priests armed with their 'rods of iron' unleash many torments including plagues and keeps them at bay as their numbers increase into the billions and to numbers that can only be referred to as the sand of the sea."

Mel, sensing that all of the information and wonder might be causing them to drift off in amazement, grabbed their attention again by saying, "Gog and his Magog nations, consist of evil beings during this time period. Gog rules the northern lands while his Magog nations rule the southern lands. They have absolute power over physical life and death of their subjects who for the most part, look up to them as some type of demi-gods, who they assume are invincible."

The Prophet Ezekiel in chapters 38 & 39 is told by God about them and their outcome. First, let's talk about **Gog**, of the land of Magog, the prince of Rosh, Meshech, and Tubal. God speaks to Ezekiel that He is against Gog, the prince of (1)Rosh, (2)Meshech, and (3) Tubal."

Tom asked, "When and how does this take place?"

Mel replied, "It's recorded that during the latter years and prior to Judgment Day, those living around the New Jerusalem will be surrounded by Gog along with his massively great evil armies, intending to invade into the land of those who were brought back from the sword. Those who were gathered from many people on the mountains of Israel, which had long been desolate were brought out of the nations, and now all of them dwell safely on God's Holy Mountains.

Ezekiel said concerning them, "*They will ascend, coming like a storm, covering the land like a cloud, you and all your troops and many peoples with you.*" *They plan to take plunder and to take booty, to stretch out your hand against the waste places that are again inhabited, and against a people gathered from the nations, who have acquired livestock and goods, who dwell in the midst of the land.*"

Maria asked, "What will they look like?"

Mel described them as follows, "They have a great army, horses, and horsemen, all splendidly clothed, a great company with bucklers and shields, all of them handling swords."

Tom then asked, "How exactly does their destruction happen?"

Mel segued in saying, "First let's discuss the more peaceful attributes of the 1000-years. Then, we'll deal with Gog and his Magog nations, pure evil."

d. ANIMALS PEACEFUL

Maria began by asking a rhetorical question, "Are all animals peaceful?"

"Part of the answer regarding the nature of the kingdom, is found in the book of Isaiah 11:6-9 It is revealed that

The wolf also shall dwell with the lamb, and
the leopard shall lie down with the kid; and
the calf and the young lion and the fatling together; and
a little child shall lead them.
And the cow and the bear shall feed; their young ones shall lie down together: and
the lion shall eat straw like the ox. And
the sucking child shall play on the hole of the asp, and
the weaned child shall put his hand on the dragon's den.
They shall not hurt nor destroy in all my holy mountain: for the earth shall be full of the knowledge of the LORD, as the waters cover the sea."

"First of all, we see that animals that are presently carnivorous, will now eat vegetation only, so that the animals will not fear one another or harm people. It will be like in the Garden of Eden, when all animals were herbivores, a time when neither man nor beast ate animal flesh."

Genesis 1:29-30 says *"And God said, Behold, I have given you every herb bearing seed, which is upon the face of all the earth, and every tree, in the which is the fruit of a tree yielding seed; to you it shall be for meat. And to every beast of the earth, and to every fowl of the air, and to everything that creepeth upon the earth, wherein there is life, I have given every green herb for meat: and it was so."*

"The Hebrew word "oklah" translated "meat" by the King James Version of the Bible (KJV) simply means food or that which is devoured. Notice that the beasts are neither given for Adam's food, nor for one another's food. Both Adam and the beasts are given the herbs and fruits to eat. So, man and beast were all vegetarians."

"However, God changed things after the great flood. In Genesis 9:2-3 God says to Noah, *'And the fear of you and the dread of you shall be upon every beast of the earth, and upon every fowl of the air, upon all that moveth upon the earth, and upon all the fishes of the sea; into your hand are they delivered. Every moving thing that liveth shall be meat for you; even as the green herb have I given you all things.'* So the animals began to fear man, because man was given permission to eat them and now many animals became carnivorous."

Joe asked a strange question to Mel by saying, "Will our pets be with us during these days?"

Mel smiled, saying, "Would it please you to see them again? If so, why not?"

Maria jumped in saying, "You mean all pets will come back?" Mel's reply explained that only those pets who touched your soul to the extent that an eternal bond was created, and to remember that love transcends death.

Tom, now very curious, said, "But animals don't have souls, do they?"

Mel's reply was, "No they don't need a soul; however, they have a 'life force' and are 'man's best friend'. Remember, people say that no one knows where the name 'dog' originated. The originator is simple, when you spell dog backwards, you know."

Joe asked when he and Maria would see their best friend Bailey.

"Look over there, tell me what you see. '' said Mel as he waved his hand.

Joe answered, "It is Maria, me and our dog Bailey, and groups of people have gathered around and it looks like we are teaching them."

Maria sighed saying, "Look, Bailey's actually speaking to us somehow."

Mel smiled saying, "As it was in the beginning, so it begins again. In Jubilees in the Apocrypha we read that in the Garden of Eden, creation could communicate.

27. And on that day on which <u>Adam went forth from the garden,</u> he offered as a sweet savour an offering, frankincense, galbanum, and stacte, and spices in the morning with the rising of the sun from the day when he covered his shame.

*28. <u>And on that day</u> **was closed the mouth** of all beasts, and of cattle, and of birds, and of whatever walketh, and of whatever moveth, so that they could no longer speak:*

for **<u>they had all spoken</u>.... <u>one with another</u>.....<u>with one lip</u>... and <u>with one tongue.</u>*

29. And He sent out of the Garden of Eden all flesh that was in the Garden of Eden, and all flesh was scattered according to its kinds, and according to its types unto the places which had been created for them."

Maria's teary eyes streamed in awe; she was speechless as to the awesomeness of God's Love.

Tom excitedly said, "Now that's a sight I never thought I'd see. Look over there it's me with the group next to you, with Sammy, my dog."

Maria, regaining some composure, asked, "Why are Joe, Me and Bailey together?"

Mel, smiled and said, "Family, certain bonds of eternal love cannot be broken, and why should they? Remember, Heaven is vastly more complex than you can possibly imagine. God's Holy mountain will contain all these loving creatures, God sees and monitors His creation all the time."

Maria looked at Joe and now both had tears in their eyes. Years ago, before Bailey died, they had touched her paw over 500 times to her offerings, given to God. After their Bailey died, they continued to pray and offer to God, for her. She and Joe even wrote a little booklet titled, 'Bailey goes to Heaven'."

Mel looked at them lovingly saying, "Everything written in your little book was true." Now all three and Mel had tears in their eyes. This was a first, for up until to then they never saw 'tears' in Mel's eyes.

Mel then gently asked, "In the morning, what sounds make you happy?"

Maria answered immediately, "The singing of the birds."

Mel said "Look, what do you see in the trees?"

"Birds." she replied. "You know if God can be so kind to His little creatures, he must have such… I can't find the proper words!"

Mel added how about, "Marvelous, infinite, love to name a few. Later, you will experience wonders so vast, they would at this moment in time, overwhelm you." Maria sighed… "Already there."

Mel added, "Later, we will discuss the 'God Sightings' in your book."

Joe asked, "Mel, when does 'later' happen?"

Mel smiled again saying, "When you tend unto the Gardens of God."

Joe replied, "You mean the stars?"

"Think bigger my friend." Mel smiled.

Tom asked, "How vast is space? Your answer was strange."

"How vast is your imagination?" replied Mel.

Tom added that scientists say it's about 20 billion years old and Mel smiled saying to him "Tom, you're still only thinking in one dimension".

Maria asked, "How many dimensions are there?"

Mel said again, "How vast is your imagination?"

Joe added; "Can you give us a little hint?"

Mel said, "When you have answered these three basic questions:

1- "Measure me the blast of the wind."

Joe, being cheeky, answered, "Anemometers monitor the blast of wind air speed. Mel, would you like the answer in imperial or metric?"

2 - "Weigh me the weight of fire."

Joe again answered, "For most 'everyday' fires, the density of the gas in the flame will be about 1/4 the density of air. So, since air (at sea level) weighs about 1300 g per cubic meter we divide this by four and get about 325 grams per cubic meter. My answer was in metric just in case you're wondering."

3- "Recall the day that has passed."

Joe concluding said, "Not only have we answered this, we have also travelled up and down the timeline with you."

Mel actually chuckled when Maria asked Joe, "How do you know such things?"

Joe replied, "I've been reading an information app on my cell phone."

Maria laughed saying, "Joe cell phones are useless now." Joe replied, "Not the data portion'."

Tom weighed in saying, "We're spiritual beings so how can you even have such an archaic device?"

Joe simply replied, "It was in my pocket. We seem to be wearing clothes, don't we?"

They seemed perplexed concerning Joe's comments.

Mel asked, "And where did that app come from Joe. Remember time-travel information was unknown to people of your time?"

Joe, looking perplexed, handed off the question to Tom who said, "It had to have come from you! Thanks Mel."

Mel continued, "Your three questions were answered, albeit in a way only Joe could accomplish. The Gardens of God are not just the stars, Joe, but uncountable galaxies and at that time, the word 'time' takes on an entirely different meaning. Remember when you said, 'Winky, Blinky and Twinkie and the last being light-speed, soon we will add more words such as googolplexy that will dwarf the former. For now, one step at a time."

Joe whispered to Maria, "I think he just made up that rhyming word."

"You thinky?" she whispered back.

Mel hushed their chatter by saying, "Now we begin discussing in more detail, the role of the "Royal Kings and Royal Priests of God. They are unique within God's Galaxies, firstlings you can say."

e. FEAST OF THE TABERNACLES

The Feast of Tabernacles takes place on the 15th of the Hebrew month Tishri. This was the seventh month on the Hebrew calendar and usually occurs in late September to mid-October.

The feast begins when the fall harvest had just been completed. It was a time of joyous celebration as the Israelites celebrated God's continued provision for them in the current harvest and remembered His provision and protection during the 40 years in the wilderness.

Maria asked, "How can all the people on earth converge upon the New Jerusalem at the same time?"

Joe then added, "Remember in olden times people only had one harvest each year, now they have a harvest each month."

"True." Mel commented; "However, the entire world is commanded by God to bring their thanksgiving offerings to Him once each year, it will be the same date as in olden times.

Now, the 'Feast of the Tabernacles', is a truly most glorious event for some, for others, not so good. As this time period begins, the saved are commanded by God to bring offerings unto Him during the yearly 'Feast of the Tabernacles.' This immediately begins the separation of the 'Wise and Foolish' all over again as the good and the bad declare and define themselves. In very short order, the bad begin to challenge the authority of God's command, reminiscent of when the band of Korah challenged Moses' authority after God's people left Egypt and went into the desert. We remember that they chose poorly, and the earth opened, and consumed them."

Maria then said, "I get it. Even though there are millions, then billons of people living on the earth, vast numbers are the anti-God, and sooner or later refuse to bring offerings to Him. So, those bringing their offerings can come to one of the 12 gates of the New Jerusalem, so everything will be in perfect harmony."

Mel replied, "Correct. Tom please read from Zechariah 14: 16-19, The Nations Worship the King."

GOD'S COMMAND

Tom began reading the following:

16 And it shall come to pass that everyone who is left of all the nations which came against Jerusalem shall go up from year to year to worship the King, the Lord of hosts, and to keep the Feast of Tabernacles. 17 And it shall be that whichever of the families of the earth do not come up to Jerusalem to worship the King, the Lord of hosts, on them there will be no rain. 18 If the family of Egypt will not come up and enter in, they shall have no rain; they shall receive the plague with which the Lord strikes the nations who do not come up to keep the Feast of Tabernacles. 19 This shall be the punishment of Egypt and the punishment of all the nations that do not come up to keep the Feast of Tabernacles.

Mel interrupted Tom saying, "You think people would have learned from their past mistakes and mistakes of others, fools though, never learn? Now the next verses are also most interesting, Tom please continue."

Tom continued:

20 In that day "HOLINESS TO THE LORD" shall be engraved on the bells of the horses. The pots in the Lord's house shall be like the bowls before the altar. 21 Yes, every pot in Jerusalem and Judah shall be holiness to the Lord of hosts. (shall be engraved "HOLINESS TO THE LORD OF HOSTS") Everyone who sacrifices shall come and take them and cook in them. In that day there shall no longer be a Canaanite in the house of the Lord of hosts.

Maria commented, "Now that will make a delightful sound for everyone to hear."

Mel gave more details concerning this time and spoke. "The bad migrate in short order away from the New Jerusalem and into the outer coastal regions."

Joe asked, "Why do people still die during these 1000 years?"

Mel replied, "Although Satan is bound, evil is still alive and well in the hearts of people. Those who migrate away from the New Jerusalem and drift to the outer zones revert back to killing of animals, people, and all manifestations of satanic evil. This is why it reads, 'a person who dies at 100 is like a child.' This means simply that if a person dies at 100 or so years of age they would be classified as incredibly young. People will not die during these days from natural causes, only if they are killed in battle, conflicts, murder, assassinations and all other satanic doings."

"There are two groups."

"The First Group, those who keep their garments pure and who have their names removed from the Judgement Day books. They subsequently have their names written into the Book of Life and live eternally."

"The Second Group, the evil-seed anti-God, from the nations of Gog and his Magog nations, who are consumed by fire, on Judgment Day."

All souls exempted from Judgement Day wear the Garments of Salvation. During the 1000-years they keep their outer and inner garments pure. They actually appear different and are immediately known by their dress code. Those of the reanimated Israel nation have clothes for their daily activities and clothes for the Sabbath and special garments worn during the 'Feast of Tabernacles'."

The good become more and more Holy and draw ever closer to their God, they make use of the time of grace.

Maria queried; "Will their physical appearance be different than what humans looked like in the past?"

Mel replied, "Yes. Remember when people saw in dreams or visions their departed loved ones? Did they appear to them as old and decrepit? No, they appeared in their prime. Adam was adult-created and so will the resurrected nation of Israel and all reanimated people be."

Maria asked, "Who are allowed to go in and out of the New Jerusalem?"

Mel interjected, "Yes as written, 'There shall by no means enter it anything that defiles, or causes an abomination or a lie, but only those who are written in the Lamb's Book of Life."

"The people of the nation's surrounding the New Jerusalem have the opportunity to bring their offerings to the New Jerusalem."

Joe asked, "Will they be allowed to enter into the walled New Jerusalem through its 12 portals?"

The reply from Mel was, "Initially, no, all living outside of the New Jerusalem, will with their horses and offerings come to the 12 portals of the New Jerusalem however only those written in the Lamb's Book of Life can enter into the New Jerusalem."

Maria asked, "Can they somehow get their names into the Lamb's Book of Life?"

"Wait and see," was all Mel added.

Maria concluded, "It seems like the third Holy Sacrament will be offered to those living outside of the New Jerusalem and if they remain faithful and loyal to God, they may be allowed to enter into it."

"So," Joe commented, "Seems like those who drifted to the coastal zones are unlikely to bring offerings to God."

Mel said, "Correct Joe, the further the distance between them and God, the more evil they became. Concerning the Feast of Tabernacles, the prophet Zechariah in chapter 14:16-19 relays what will happen to the Gentile nations NOT keeping the feast of tabernacles during these days.

"And it shall come to pass, that every one that is left of all the nations which came against Jerusalem shall even go up from year to year to worship the King, the LORD of hosts, and to keep the feast of tabernacles. And it shall be, that whoso will not come up of all the families of the earth unto Jerusalem to worship the King, the LORD of hosts, even upon them shall be no rain. And if the family of Egypt go not up, and come not, that have no rain; there shall be the plague, wherewith the LORD will smite the heathen that come not up to keep the feast of tabernacles. This shall be the punishment of Egypt, and the punishment of all nations that come not up to keep the feast of tabernacles."

The first punishment is 'No rain.'

The second is 'The plague.'

Joe asked, "When do the plagues begin?"

Mel's answer was quick, "They commence upon the conclusion of the Feast of Tabernacles and that's just for starters."

Mel said to the three of them, "Did you notice that these evil-seeds are also called 'the heathen'."

Maria asked, "But didn't they all get 'Garments of Salvation', so why are they called heathens?"

"Remember," Mel replied, "They were admonished to keep their garments pure. Failing which, they lose them. We are also looking forward, years and centuries into the future, the initial 'saved' had such garments however their offspring do not. All subsequent births must be baptized by those authorized by God during these days. Since evil separates, baptisms cease."

"Here we see that in the 1000-Year Kingdom, all the 'saved' namely those living who surround the New Jerusalem, being the 12 tribes of Israel and then all the 'heathens' that surround them, must keep the feast of tabernacles or suffer the consequences. Remember God said in Ezekiel 43:7, "And he said unto me, Son of man, the place of my throne, and the place of the soles of my feet, where I will dwell in the midst of the children of Israel forever, and my holy name, shall the house of Israel no more defile."

Mel concluded by saying, "During these days, as recorded in Zechariah 8:22-23, people will cleave to the Godly and actually desire salvation. Up to now they may only have heard about God and have not experienced God." "Thus says the Lord of hosts: 'In those days ten men from every language of the nations shall grasp the sleeve of a Jewish man, saying, "Let us go with you, for we have heard that God is with you."

Chapter Twenty-Two:

DANIEL'S VISION OF THE BEASTS

Mel said, "Now a little history. 15 months prior to the Judgment Day destruction of Gog, his Magog armies and peoples, there will come 3 beasts. We actually must discuss 4 beasts who are actually three in order to understand who the helpers of Satan are when he is released for a little while. No, I'm not making a funny, just teasing you a little. Now Daniel had a vision of the four beasts in chapter 7: 4-6"

"The first was like a lion and had eagle's wings. I watched till its wings were plucked off and it was lifted up from the earth and made to stand on two feet like a man, and a man's heart was given to it."

"The second was like a bear. It was raised up on one side and had three ribs in its mouth between its teeth. And they said thus to it 'Arise, devour much flesh!'"

"The third was like a leopard which had on its back four wings of a bird. The beast also had four heads, and dominion was given to it."

"The fourth had 10 horns. It had huge iron teeth, it was devouring, breaking in pieces, and trampling the residue with its feet. It was different from all the beasts that were before it, and it had ten horns. I was considering the horns, and there was another horn, a little one, coming up among them, before whom three of the first horns were plucked out by the roots. And there, in this horn, were eyes like the eyes of a man, and a mouth speaking pompous words."

Mel paraphrased, "This fourth beast was the 'Sea Beast' who engenders the 'Land Beast' so there are two in one, you might say

'Twin Beasts' and that's why the false prophet always does his deceiving wonders in the presence of the sea beast. As Tom used to say, this is a furtive discovery for you, not me. The false prophet was an evil human which made him bad but powerless and only with the power from the beast did he appear to be great. And actually, the sea beast received his power from his father Satan."

"I don't know if you caught this fact that Satan with his three beast entities always copies God's Holy Trinity.

The 'twin beasts' are slain and given to the burning flame. Concerning their deaths, it is recorded in the book of Revelation 19:19-21 that the (false president) the sea beast was captured, and with him the (false prophet) the land beast who worked signs in his presence, by which he deceived those who received the mark of the beast and those who worshiped his image. These two were cast alive into the lake of fire burning with brimstone."

"See? The false president and false prophet are both caught and cast into the lake of fire. This is what people refer to as hell, and it's a one-way trip.

Now we come to the three remaining beasts mentioned in Daniel 9:12 they had their dominion taken away, yet their lives were prolonged for a season and a time. A season is 3 months and a time is 12 months, together they total 15 months."

"These three beasts are those three demons that went out to deceive the 10 kings and their soldiers prior to Armageddon. The question may be asked, are these the same three beasts that once again deceive the people just prior to Armageddon? Yes!"

THREE BEASTS RELEASED

Mel commented, "The three deceiving beasts (demons) that I just told you about were captured but not cast, just yet, into the lake of fire. They still serve a purpose and are loosened 15 months prior Judgement Day. These demons go out to the evil rulers and the people that by now number in the billions.

During the 1000-Year Kingdom all people must still remain faithful and not lose their garments of salvation. God said to the people as recorded in the Bible in Job, not to listen to Satan's soft and cunning words of promise. Humans seem to always want to learn the hard way and once again as the sand of the sea, turn and follow Satan. Learning the hard way this time results in spiritual death."

Mel again said, "Also, just prior to the destruction of Gog, his Magog armies, his anti-God people, and Judgment Day, Satan is loosed for a while. This time period corresponds to the same 15 months when the 3 beasts were released."

We will now read about this.

CHAPTER TWENTY-THREE:

RISE OF GOG
AND HIS MAGOG NATIONS

el began, "Now history repeats itself for the last time. 'Gog and his Magog nations are very evil anti-God people. From the north to the south. Picture the north, consisting of the upper portion, with its temperatures ranging from moderate to cold and harsh. The south, the lower portion, being the same. In total, they occupy most of the earth's land mass. Similar to the north and south climates prior on earth.

Remember there were <u>millions of people brought back to life</u> to work out their soul salvation. It is recorded that their final head count will number like the sand of the sea, meaning billions upon billions. Bear in mind that God does not remove His love for them, they do this themselves by their own actions.

Mel added that also in Revelation 22: 14 we read, "<u>Blessed are those who do His commandments</u> that they may have the right to the tree of life and <u>may enter through the gates into the city</u>. 15 Living Bible (TLB) "Outside the city are those who have strayed away from God, and the sorcerers and the immoral and murderers and idolaters, and all who love to lie, and do so.

Tom asked, "Can you explain, please?"

a. BLESSED ARE THOSE WHO DO HIS COMMAND-MENTS
b. THE RIGHT TO THE TREE OF LIFE

c. MAY ENTER THROUGH THE GATES INTO THE CITY

"Very good questions." replied Mel, "Let's delve into them in more detail. These are the saved, those brought back to mortal life requiring salvation and comprising of the following."

d. THE ARMY NATION OF ISRAEL, reanimated from their dry bones by God, in human bodies.

e. GOD WILL HAVE MERCY ON THE WHOLE HOUSE OF ISREAL

In Ezekiel 39 *"Therefore thus says the Lord God: 'Now I will bring back the captives of Jacob, and have **mercy on the whole house of Israel;** and I will be jealous for My holy name—after they have borne their shame, and all their unfaithfulness in which they were unfaithful to Me, when they dwelt safely in their own land and no one made them afraid. When I have brought them back from the peoples and gathered them out of their enemies' lands, and I am hallowed in them in the sight of many nations, then they shall know that I am the Lord their God, who sent them into captivity among the nations, but also brought them back to their land, and left none of them captive any longer. <u>And I will not hide My face from them anymore; **for I shall have poured out My Spirit on the house of Israel,'** says the Lord God.</u>"*

f. The GOOD, wearing their Marriage garments, from the Kings Feast, in human bodies,

g. The BAD, wearing their Marriage garments deceitfully 'remember the evil-seeds', from the Kings Feast, in human bodies, mind-you they soon shed these garments as they felt uncomfortable in them, in the first place and only took them out of fear.

The above live in 12 tribes adjacent to the four-sides of the New Jerusalem having King David as their leader. All others surround them, and soon many begin migrating farther and farther away to the coastal areas.

**Take note, when God says
"Have mercy on the whole house of Israel"
this means all of His human creation from Adam and Eve.**

At first all obey God's commandment. Those who remain true and faithful to their God, after receiving the three Holy Sacraments, will be allowed during the 'Feast of the Tabernacles' to bring their offerings, through the gates and into the New Jerusalem, however only the Royal Kings can bring them into God's Temple. Also bear in mind that there is no physical temple at this time for God and Jesus are the Temple, one might say the Temple now is Spiritual."

Tom added, "Now it begins to make sense to me, those Israelites living around the New Jerusalem have the opportunity to mature in faith and if so, they will be allowed to bring their offerings into the New Jerusalem. This also extends to those who live that surround the 12 Tribes of Israel. What do you think Mel?"

Maria asked, "Can you give us a number as to how many initially surround the 12 tribes?

Joe commented, "Maria, the Bible already gives us the answer 'as the sand of the sea'"

Mel answered, "Perfect answer Joe.

Mel continued, God wants all to be saved, for purity is absolute. However, this also brings to mind another matter, the evil-seeds descendants born during the Kingdom of Peace Time, never witnessed Armageddon. Evil teaches them, it was a lie and that the past events had a different outcome. These descendants see their parents as superior beings who were victorious and unaffected by the battle Armageddon.

These evil seeds germinate, become rooted, grow and congregate in all areas of the recombined earth, consisting of Gog and his Magog nations. The Bible says they occupy the lands in the 4 corners of the earth. Satan although in prison, is alive and well within their souls.

Those born to evil-seed parents begin worshiping idols, demons, and Satan. Generation after generation these EVIL-SEEDS grow into vast numbers joining as recorded in the Bible the "Sand of the sea".

The Royal Kings and Royal Priests of God must constantly keep these satanic hordes in check and skirmishes occur frequently. People once again turn to Satan's evil ways, knowingly or unknowingly, and begin multiplying in alarming rates. Again, plagues are unleashed upon evil and the Children of God armed with the 'rods of iron' keep them at bay.

Mel clasped his hands together and continued, "It does not take long for evil to take root. My old friend and Prophet Isaiah says in Isaiah 65:17-25 *for behold, I create new heavens and a new earth. And the former shall not be remembered or come to mind. But be glad and rejoice forever in what I create for behold, I create Jerusalem as a rejoicing, and her people a joy. I will rejoice in Jerusalem, and joy in My people the voice of weeping shall no longer be heard in her, Nor the voice of crying.* "*No more shall an infant from there live but a few days, Nor an old man who has not fulfilled his days; For the child shall die one hundred years old,*

a. *But the sinner being one hundred years old shall be accursed.*
b. *They shall build houses and inhabit them.*
c. *They shall plant vineyards and eat their fruit.*
d. *They shall not build and another inhabit.*
e. *They shall not plant and another eat.*
f. *For as the days of a tree, so shall be the days of My people.*
g. *And My elect shall long enjoy the work of their hands. They shall not labor in vain,*
h. *Nor bring forth children for trouble. For they shall be the descendants of the blessed of the Lord, and their offspring with them.*
i. *"It shall come to pass That before they call, I will answer and while they are still speaking, I will hear.*
j. *The wolf and the lamb shall feed together.*
k. *The lion shall eat straw like the ox.*
l. *And dust shall be the serpent's food.*
m. *They shall not hurt nor destroy in all My holy mountain," Says the Lord.*

God creates a New Heaven and Earth. Should a person die at the age of 100 (here is wisdom, all deaths that occur during the 1000-years will not be of natural causes, for only evil-kills) and they would be referred to as a 'child'. There will be no rich land rulers as everyone will work and reap the benefits of their labors. Mothers will give birth to their children without distress, anxiety, or danger.

Most Christians have heard what follows next at some time during their lives, 'The wolf and the lamb shall feed together, the lion shall eat straw like the ox. And dust shall be the serpent's food.'

Mel commented "'They shall not hurt nor destroy in all My holy mountain,' says the Lord."

Mel looked at them quizzically and said, "In 'all my holy mountain', refers to the area within the walls of the New Jerusalem. Within the walls is peace. The further you travel outside the walls… everything but peace, so this is where the evil live. Also, within the New Jerusalem, the word 'death' has no place. Subsequently, those who are allowed to bring their offerings unto God receive access to the 'Tree of Life,' and never die."

"The 1000-Years are given so that souls can have a new and eternal beginning. It is a time of peace intended for all to focus upon their soul-salvation without interference from evil, and the pressures of life. Those living are given the opportunity to draw close to their God and receive His blessings. It is incomprehensible that the vast majority reject the mercy and salvation offered unto them."

"Now, let's look at how the evil-seeds once again germinate into weeds. Also, bear in mind that in addition to the evil-seeds there are billions of reanimated people who are given a second chance for salvation who also develop, into the anti-God."

"Remember that all people are commanded by God to attend the 'Feast of the Tabernacles' each year."

"During the early years, in addition to the 12 Tribes having David as their king, some of them along with other evil-hearted people begin to migrate outwards, and also gather and form into tribes. Soon these tribes begin to compete with each other, for territory rights and dominance. As a result, they steadily move to the 4-corners of the earth or one could say the top and bottom halves of the earth."

"These tribes have leaders, reminiscent of the band of Korah, who along with a large number of others revolted very early during their sojourn against Moses of past times. Remember they were those who were swallowed by the earth for they chose poorly."

"Initially all obeyed God's command, some wholeheartedly and others obeyed only out of fear that turned into hate. A progression whereby the bad moved further and further away from the good begins to take place and, gathers momentum very quickly. They do not want to be told what to do, rather they want power over people themselves".

"Their hearts again grow cold towards their God even though they can see Heaven on earth and are witnesses to a most glorious time-period. Soon they decide not to bring offerings to God, as commanded."

"Their failure to bring offerings to God causes a drought. In order to support themselves they gravitate towards the coastal regions of the great global ocean called the Great Sea. To grasp an easy picture of this, consider the rejoined land masses now as one large continent roughly circular in size having the New Jerusalem at its center."

"The droughts create a barrier between the good and the bad. As time progresses this barrier becomes massive in its size and comes to be known as the "dead zone". Once the foolish anti-God migrate through the dead zone, their fate is sealed. Many of the anti-God migrate far away to the coastal regions to the north and south hemispheres. Some of them only migrate a shorter distance in the belief that they can sneak up and plunder those living in peace surrounding the New Jerusalem. Big mistake. Those foolish enough to attempt attacking the Israelites and their surrounding neighbors will encounter the Royal Kings equipped with the 'rods of iron' capable of unleashing pure terror that panics and sends them scattering back to their sad places of dwelling, for a while."

Maria asked; "Why do they keep returning in a vain attempt to loot and plunder?"

Mel responded, "They become wild, they do not want to labor, plant crops or do anything but steal. This is one reason that they fight amongst themselves, stealing, looting, killing and worse becoming their norm. To answer your question fully, they become barbaric."

"Over time, the ungodly develop into two groups having the evil-possessed Gog as their supreme ruler and his Magog nations. Gog, via his commanders, controls all the areas of the rejoined land-masses in the 4 corners of the earth, again being the two hemispheres."

"As the sand of the sea, these evil-seeds again take root, participating in everything ungodly. Satan, although in prison, is alive and well within their souls. The hearts and souls of the vast majority of people once again turn to satanically wicked ways resulting in death, sickness, hate and all things evil."

"Yes, Satan is bound and unable to directly influence mankind, however, soon the bad migrate away from the New Jerusalem to the outer zones that have the great sea as its border. Those who migrate to the outer zones are evil, Satan's seeds and their descendants."

"The further away from the New Jerusalem you go the more influence Gog, and his Magog leaders have over the anti-God. Their colors are **Gold, Blue and Purple**. The Prophet Ezekiel talks about Gog and his Magog forces, known as the Anti-God.

Tom added, "Once while in England I went to the Guildhall in London. There I saw two giant statues representing Gog and Magog, leaders of the races of giants, and who are mentioned in the Book of Revelations. When I looked up the dictionary meaning as to the meaning of Gog the definition stated that Gog, is the supreme ruler controlling all areas and having his commanders controlling the people of his Magog areas or nations, as mentioned in Rev. 20:8. Gog and his Magog commanders are anti-God, who come under the dominion of Satan. Again, they are barbaric.

They were very large people similar to that of the Biblical Goliath. Each was attired in brilliant and colorful colors of Gold, Blue and Purple. Their appearance was most intimidating, and I wondered as to why they were on display, seems certain factions deemed them noteworthy. England has an evil history and is linked to them."

Maria said, "Evil has been around since the angels were cast out of Heaven and then became known as the 'fallen angels. They have one agenda and that is to promote the hell that permeates from within them. We know that their existence is drawing to an end, perhaps they cannot fathom such a termination. This is one reason why they never cease perpetuating their anti-God agenda. 'Misery loves company.'"

Tom asked, "From what I remember God created man in His image."

"Yes," replied Mel, "In Genesis chapter 1, *Then God said, "Let Us make man in Our image, according to Our likeness; let them have dominion over the fish of the sea, over the birds of the air, and over the cattle, over all the earth and over every creeping thing that creeps on the earth." 27 So God created man in His own image; in the image of God He created him; male and female He created them.*

And in 'Genesis 2 *it is written, and God blessed the seventh day, and sanctified it: because that in it he had rested from all his work which God created and made. These are the generations of the heavens and of the earth when they were created, in the day that the Lord God made the earth and the heavens."*

Take special note, God said, "*Let Us make man in Our image, according to Our likeness. "God also breathed into his nostrils the breath of life; and man became a living soul."*

8 *And the Lord God planted a garden eastward in Eden; and there he put the man whom he had formed.*

Now, Adam and Eve lived in the Garden Section of Eden in its Easterly Area.

Remember after Cain killed Abel he was banished from the Garden of Eden.

God said in Genesis chapter 4.

4:11 *So now you are cursed from the earth, which has opened its mouth to receive your brother's blood from your hand.*
12 *When you till the ground, it shall no longer yield its strength to you.*

"***A fugitive and a vagabond you shall be on the earth***."

13 And Cain said to the Lord, "My punishment is greater than I can bear!

14 Surely You have driven me out this day from the face of the ground; I shall be hidden from Your face; I shall be a fugitive and a vagabond on the earth,

and it will happen that anyone who finds me will kill me."

15 And the Lord said to him, "Therefore, whoever kills Cain, vengeance shall be taken on him sevenfold."

And the Lord set a mark on Cain, lest anyone finding him should kill him.

16 Then Cain went out from the presence of the Lord and dwelt in the land of Nod, outside of Eden, further to the east.

We read in, Jubilees 4:9 which narrates that Cain settled down and married his sister Awan, who bore his first son, the first Enoch, approximately 196 years after the creation of Adam.

And Cain took Âwân his sister to be his wife and she bare him Enoch at the close of the fourth jubilee. And in the first year of the first week of the fifth jubilee, houses were built on the earth, and Cain built a city, and called its name after the name of his son Enoch.

"Now listen closely." Mel whispered.

"The creation of Adam and Eve having a higher status than Satan was Satan's downfall, his ego could not comprehend God's plan. Remember up to now there were beings upon earth namely, races referred to as, Leviathan and Enoch, the first lived in the Jungles and the latter in the higher elevations. These were races of beings having no soul and who some loosely say were called 'cave-man.'

Adam and Eve were to be lords of God's creation and bring all beings not having soul-life to the understanding of God and His creation. Bear in mind that these people from the past were not ignorant, overtime they had come to the realization that something higher must have created them and everything surrounding them.

Some may say 'How can it be that there were other people on earth at the time of Adam and Eve?' We must bear in mind that these beings were not created in the image of God, however God loves His entire creation, and everything has a purpose.

Cain knew of the "Land of Nod" and its inhabitants. The Bible reads that Cain went to this land referred to as "Nod" <u>to the east of the Garden of Eden.</u>

Remember at this time Adam and Eve had sinned
and that angered God; thus, they were expelled
from the Garden of Eden.

Mel continued to whisper, "Consider this, was the speaking serpent and the forbidden apple-fruit actual or were they metaphors, (one tidbit of information, a Catholic Bishop arbitrarily deemed it an apple, for the Bible never mentioned, what the forbidden fruit was).

Did Adam and Eve speak to these people while in the Garden of Eden, and if so, what did they discuss or do? I will simply say that whatever they said or did, caused them to be evicted from the Garden of Eden, and possibly caused the people from the Land of Nod to hate them, and their children, namely Cain, who by virtue of the tilling of the fields came into their proximity. And where did the evil killing thought that entered Cain come from, certainly not from God?

In addition to Cain knowing about the "Land of Nod", he knew of the people living there.

He said to God, "*That anyone who finds me will kill me.*" Cain must have encountered the people from the "Land of Nod" eastward of the Garden of Eden, during the tilling of his fields. These people must have been angered by the appearance of Cain; this indicates that the physical appearance of Cain was different. Perhaps there were differences in size, color, speech etc. It would seem plausible that there must have also been some type of <u>barrier</u> separating them so they could not simply chase and kill Cain for God had to place a mark on Cain to protect him from them.

Maria suggested, "Perhaps the land within Eden was more fertile and no bugs and this is why those outside were jealous of the bountiful crops within."

"Imagine if these people did not have soul-life yet and what if Satan had manipulated them into giants or people having other traits. Adam and Eve were to educate them in due time and bring them soul-life. To the consternation of Satan, man was created having the ultimate status of having 'body, soul and spirit' like God. Angels were a spiritual creation having no physical body or soul. This is not a put down rather each had different functions within God's plan."

"Satan was instructed that he and the angels were to serve man. Satan took this as an insult, but he should have trusted God and looked after Adam and Eve as a mother would her children. Satan's plan was to destroy the relationship between Adam, Eve and God, he succeeded. Satan became furious, hateful and spiteful and he decided to revolt and leave the presence of God. One third of the angels numbering 200 million also sided with him and all were expelled from Heaven and the presence of God."

Joe asked an open-ended question, "Did Satan sow evil-seeds throughout the universe after he decided not to obey God's command?"

Tom replied, "I did read somewhere that of the fallen angels, 200 descended to the earth and took human beautiful females, impregnated them and giants came forth."

Mel deflected his question saying, "Evil-seeds have no boundaries, there will be much house-cleaning you might say." Mel left it at that.

Maria asked, "Please elaborate."

One word resounded from the Heavens, "Soon" and it did not originate from Mel!

Mel then said, "With respect to Gog and his Magog nations, let's move forward."

CHAPTER TWENTY-FOUR

SATAN LOOSED FOR A WHILE
(15 months)

el reiterated, "Towards the end of the 1000-years Satan is loosed from his confinement pit for 15 months.

Also, at this time his 3-demons as described in the book of Daniel are also released for 15 months. We read in Daniel 7:11-12 'I watched then because of the sound of the pompous words which the horn was speaking; I watched till the beast was slain, and its body destroyed and given to the burning flame.'

**As for the rest of the beasts,
they had their dominion taken away,
<u>yet their lives were prolonged for a season and a time</u>.**

Mel continued saying, "A ''season' is 12 months and a 'time' is 3 months and that these total 15 months. So, we see that Satan and his 3-demons are given 15 months to once again go to the people to rile them into a frenzy, and to gather them for "The Cull of the Damned Judgment Day". This time he gathers so many the Bible says their number is as the 'sand of the sea'."

"In the book of Revelation 20: 7-8 we read."

7 Now when the thousand years have expired, <u>Satan will be released from his prison</u>

"At the end of the 1000 years we see that Satan is released."

8 and will go out to deceive the nations which are in the <u>four corners</u> of the earth, Gog and Magog, to gather them together to battle, whose number is as the <u>sand of the sea</u>.

"The four corners being the upper and lower halves of earth occupied by Gog and his Magog forces and nations."

"Satan's intent is to deceive, rile up, gather and prepare vast numbers for war or more correctly 'oblivion'."

"The Dragon released, wastes no time and immediately goes to his evil-seeds. Remember the 'bad' ushered into the King's Feast-Hall. These people were in Jerusalem, after it crumbled into oblivion, who fled into the new 'Valley of Olives' and who were picked up by the Kings forces. They accepted God's grace, only out of fear."

Mel said, "Remember all living in the 1000-Year Kingdom still had to remain true to God. During these days' vast numbers of people, once again turn their backs on God. The anti-God will number in the billions and another epic battle soon occurs."

"Also, during these 1000 years, many plagues are directed at the anti-God, (not zombie plagues) there will also be constant skirmishes as the Royal Kings ruling with their RODS OF IRON who constantly have to unleash energy of various types to push back the anti-God that are growing in vast numbers."

"During these days, there will be fantastic Godly happenings centered around the New Jerusalem, there will be many mysteries of God, explained however all this this did not stop evil from growing."

Joe added; "People are so evil, that even after witnessing all of God's love and miracles, they still turn to Satan…you simply can't make this stuff up, as to how wicked, people really are."

Tom then said; "God gave his human creation 'free-will' and one may think this was their downfall when actually it's their greatest asset, when properly applied."

CHAPTER TWENTY-FIVE:

SATAN GATHERS HIS ARMIES

el began by saying, "In the past Satan had myriads, 200 million to be exact, of followers that were the fallen angels. Now, towards the end of the 1000-years his forces mostly consist of humans. He knows that there is not even a remote chance in hell, that he will have victory. His evil intent is simply to take as many souls into oblivion with him, as possible. To Satan this is his last and final act of hatred towards his creator, and he considers all the misery of the past to be justified. In his mind, he felt betrayed when God made man, and he feared that man would be more exalted than he in the eyes of God. His ego got the best of him; he should have trusted God, but he chose poorly."

"Remember the old-adage, 'Misery loves company' so sad, so true, for some. Satan rallies his followers, and they will soon surround the New Jerusalem, the Israelite Nation living surrounding it and millions of the 'saved' people of God, encompassing them."

"Satan along with his 3-demons prepare them for their last battle resulting in their oblivion. This is their Judgment Day, and as previously said some time ago, "the cull of the dammed." Remember God takes no joy to see His creation that has devolved into such an ungodly state."

"Satan, upon his release from the pit, doesn't need a lot of time, just a little while to gather his anti-God for the second time. There will still be those of the evil-seeds that have during these past years facilitated people into turning away from God and as the sand of the sea."

"The Bible refers to them as, …
a. But the cowardly,
b. unbelieving,
c. abominable,
d. murderers,
e. sexually immoral,
f. sorcerers,
g. idolaters,
h. and all liars
… shall have their part in the lake which burns with fire and brimstone, which is the second death."

"Mel further commented that God actually admonished the people to not allow themselves to be deceived ever again by the Great Red Dragon, remember we already discussed this in the book of Job when God says,

WILL HE MAKE MANY SUPPLICATIONS TO YOU?
WILL HE SPEAK SOFTLY TO YOU?
WILL HE MAKE A COVENANT WITH YOU?
REMEMBER THE BATTLE—NEVER DO IT AGAIN!

Mel said, "Do you see how Satan did everything above before Armageddon, and now one thousand years later repeats them. Remember that old saying about, 'history repeating itself'? One would think that people learned from their mistakes, guess not!"

"The end to his soldiers and peoples comes quickly, and their destruction is not by human hands, rather from the plagues of destruction cast down upon them."

"The devil, who deceived them, along with his 3-demons, were cast into the lake of fire and brimstone where the beast and the false prophet are. And they will be tormented day and night forever and ever."

Mel added, "We read in Ezekiel 39 what happens to these ungodly people."

17 "And as for you, son of man, thus says the Lord God, 'Speak to every <u>sort of bird</u> and to <u>every beast of the field:</u>
"Assemble yourselves and come;

Gather together from all sides to My sacrificial meal
Which I am sacrificing for you,
A great sacrificial meal on the mountains of Israel,
That you may eat flesh and <u>drink blood</u>.

18
You shall eat the flesh of the mighty,
<u>Drink the blood</u> of the <u>princes of the earth,</u>
Of rams and lambs,
Of goats and bulls,
All of them fatlings of Bashan.

19
You shall eat fat till you are full,
<u>And drink blood till you are drunk,</u>
At My sacrificial meal
Which I am sacrificing for you.

20
You shall be filled at My table
With horses and riders,
With mighty men
And with all the men of war," says the Lord God.

Mel moved on, but first rhetorically said something strange.

1. "What type of birds or beasts of the fields would be capable of drinking blood?
2. Why did their animals also have to die?
3. In what manner did death come to the people, and animals?
4. He gave no answer but said, 'the answer is a mystery until the appointed time.'"

CHAPTER TWENTY-SIX:

GOG & HIS MAGOG ARMIES, ATTACK ISRAEL

el said; "Let's explore Gog a bit further. During the 1000-Years evil flourishes, Gog and his Magog commanders along with their forces and followers, once again forgot or ignored God's cautionary command from the days prior to Armageddon. God said concerning Satan, *"Sorrow dances before him, will he speak softly to you? Will he make a covenant with you? Remember the battle—Never do it again! He is king over all the children of pride."*

"By this late time during the 1000-Year kingdom, evil has spread across and dominates the upper and lower portions of earth. There are no weapons in the beginning of the kingdom, however, the evil-seeds soon begin making and teaching their followers how to make swords and other weapons. They make millions upon millions of swords, shields and weapons of diverse kinds. In contrast the 'good' people living around the New Jerusalem 'beat such former weapons into plows and instruments for farming.'"

"The newer generations do not believe the past battle of Armageddon's outcome, and are told it was just propaganda. Evil is alive and well and growing quickly."

"As time moves forward, people move backwards, away from God. Groups initially numbering in the tens of millions increase dramatically in population, again as the 'sand of the sea'.

"These evil people, over time, have allowed Satan to permeate their souls. They hate the New Jerusalem, and those living around it. The Godly have and need no weapons themselves, for their safety comes from the Royal Kings and Priests of God who rule with the "Rod of Iron."

God will deal with Gog and his Magog armies and soon they are destroyed by Him using various methods of destruction

<u>GOG</u>

WILL BE DESTROYED, LEAVING THEIR BODIES FOR THE BIRDS AND BEASTS TO DEVOUR.

<u>MAGOG</u>

WILL BE DESTROYED BY FIRE, LEAVING NOTHING BUT ASHES.

Now, we will discuss the specifics of these events in greater detail.

Let's read what the Prophet Ezekiel has to say, we will first read the account, and then I will elaborate on some portions, first we deal with.

Tom enquired, "Why so much Biblical history?"

Mel's answer, "So no one can ever say they were not for-told of these events."

Let's continue.

GOG
Ezekiel 38 NKJV

Ezekiel said, "Now the word of the Lord came to me, saying"

2 "Son of man, set your face against <u>Gog</u>, of the land of Magog, the prince of Rosh, Meshech, and Tubal, and prophesy against him, 3 and say, 'Thus says the Lord God: Behold, I am against you, O Gog, the prince of Rosh, Meshech, and Tubal. 4 I will turn you around, put hooks into your jaws, and lead you out, with all your
    a. *army,*
    b. *horses, and*
    c. *horsemen, all splendidly clothed,*

d. a great company with bucklers and shields,

e. all of them handling swords.

f. 5 Persia, Ethiopia, and Libya are with them, all of them with shield and helmet;

g. 6 Gomer and all its troops; the house of Togarmah from the far north and all its troops—many people are with you.

Notes

1. Gog, resides in the <u>northern hemisphere</u> where is it gets very cold the more northward you go.
2. Gog, has a great army, and his forces consist of a vast number of troops.
3. Gog, has many horses and horsemen, fully equipped with instruments of war, for horses in those days would be equal to a motorized assault army today.
4. Gog, in addition to these troops there are also many people (infantry) with them.

7 "Prepare yourself and be ready, you and all your companies that are gathered about you; and be a guard for them. 8 **<u>After many days you will be visited</u>**. In the **<u>latter years,</u>** you will come into the land of those brought back from the sword and gathered from many people <u>on the mountains of Israel,</u> which had long been desolate; <u>they were brought out of the nations,</u> and now all of them dwell safely. 9 You will ascend, coming like a storm, covering the land like a cloud, <u>you and all your troops</u> and <u>many peoples with you.</u>"

Note, the second line…. after many days, you will be visited… in the latter years.

This means, when the 1000-Year Kingdom draws to fulfillment, for 15 months, Gog and his Magog forces will be visited by the now released Great Red Dragon, Satan. Also, his 3-demons now rile these evil people, to prepare to attack God's people living around the New Jerusalem.

10 'Thus says the Lord God: "On that day it shall come to pass <u>that thoughts will arise in your mind,</u> and <u>you will make an evil plan:</u>

11 You will say, 'I will go up against a land of unwalled villages; I will go to a peaceful people, who dwell safely, all of them dwelling without walls, and having neither bars nor gates'—

*12 to take plunder and to take booty, to stretch out your hand against the waste places that are again inhabited, and against a people gathered from the nations, who have acquired livestock and goods, **who dwell in the midst of the land.** 13 Sheba, Dedan, the merchants of Tarshish, and all their young lions will say to you, 'Have you come to take plunder? Have you gathered your army to take booty, to carry away silver and gold, to take away livestock and goods, to take great plunder?'"*

Notes

1. The evil thoughts originate from the 3-demons and enter the mind of Gog and his Magog forces, for up to now they did not dare consider an attack against the Israelite nation and others, living around the New Jerusalem.

2. In addition to these demons influencing Gog and his Magog forces, they instill the thoughts that with the help of their god Satan, war with those living around the New Jerusalem is not only possible, but also now winnable.

3. There are millions/billions of the 'saved' surrounding the Israelite Nation, who during these days have come to the understanding and maturity in faith. They have received the 3 Holy Sacraments and have remained loyal to God.

4. The area of the New Jerusalem and the lands surrounding it, is referred to as being 'in the midst of the land', and evil flourishes on all its four sides.

14 "Therefore, son of man, prophesy and say to Gog, 'Thus says the Lord God: "On that day when My people Israel dwell safely, will you not know it? 15 Then you will come from your place out of the far north, you and many peoples with you, all of them riding on horses, a great company and a mighty army. 16 You will come up against My people Israel like a cloud, to cover the land. It will be in the latter days that I will bring you against My land, so that the nations may know Me, when I am hallowed in you, O Gog, before their eyes." 17 Thus says the Lord God: "Are you he of whom I have spoken in former days by My servants the prophets of Israel, who prophesied for years in those days that I would bring you against them?

Notes
1. From the <u>far north</u> they advance upon the mountains of God.
2. The New Jerusalem's land footprint is over 1500 miles square. There are many mountains within it and numerous mountains surrounding it where the 12 Tribes of Israel and those living in peace surrounding them live.
3. At this time their expanded land area is massive.
4. As we prior discussed, imagine the initial size being 1500 miles square then 2,000 miles circular and finally 2500 miles circular.
5. Initially, these millions now 1000 years later, one can imagine how vast these numbers will have increased to billions and billions.
6. They come on horses along with vast numbers of foot soldiers.
7. Their numbers so vast they create huge clouds of dust

Mel added, "Do you think the land's surface area causing the 'huge clouds of dust' is that of forests or barren scrub lands, remember this area separating the good from the bad is called the 'dead zone' for a good reason?"

"As we have previously read, his army is,
1. splendidly clothed, having multi colors, bucklers, shields
2. Helmets
3. All of them handling swords
4. Also included are those from his Magog regions of Persia, Ethiopia, and Libya."

CHAPTER TWENTY-SEVEN:

GOG and his MAGOG ARMIES DESTROYED

"**I**n the book of Revelation 20: 9-10 we read.

9 They went up on the breadth of the earth and surrounded the camp of the saints and the beloved city. And fire came down from God out of heaven and devoured them.
10 The devil, who deceived them, was cast into the lake of fire and brimstone where the beast and the false prophet are. And they will be tormented day and night forever and ever.

GOG'S ARMIES DESTROYED

Mel continued, "Read the following very carefully; "*They went up on the breadth of the earth and surrounded the camp of the saints and the beloved city.*"

Now he said, "Can you mentally visualize how huge Gog and his Magog forces were? See, they surrounded not only the New Jerusalem, the 12 Tribes of Israel and the redeemed who are those souls brought back to life from Adam and Eve who are given the opportunity for soul salvation and who have acquired the Holy Sacraments. Of this group some stayed, to their eternal joy and some migrated to the areas of Gog and Magog, to their eternal death. surrounded them. As we have already mentioned a circle over 2500 miles. Now Gog and his Magog forces forms a huge circle around them.

Joe added, "Can you imagine how vast an army it would take to actually encompass it. The Bible says 'as the sand of the sea' meaning, billions upon billions."

"Later, I will discuss their massive numbers another way, but for now, here's a tidbit of information. After Gog and his Magog forces have been killed, there will be so much wood gathered-up from their former weapons, it will supply the Godly with wood for their fires for SEVEN years."

"Consider this, people use wood for fire to cook their food, so how vast must this collected wood be, to supply all wood for millions upon millions of God's people, for SEVEN years, it would boggle your minds."

Now we read

You will come up against My people Israel like a cloud, to cover the land.

This takes place just prior to Judgment Day.

1 "And you, son of man, prophesy against Gog, and say, 'Thus says the Lord God: "Behold, I am against you, O Gog, the prince of Rosh, Meshech, and Tubal;

2 And I will turn you around and lead you on, bringing you up from the far north, and bring you against the mountains of Israel.

3 Then I will knock the bow out of your left hand, and cause the arrows to fall out of your right hand.

4 You shall fall upon the mountains of Israel, you and all your troops and the peoples who are with you. I will give you to birds of prey of every sort and to the beasts of the field to be devoured.

The leader of the Anti-God is a demonically possessed man who takes the name of Gog. The demon possessing him is also called Gog, mentioned by Ezekiel in ancient times. You can see now how this man's name comes into being. He controls his armies from the north and his soldiers and peoples from the south referred to as his Magog troops and peoples. They have bows and arrows, plus others tagging along in hopes of plunder booty. God allows the birds of prey of every sort and the beasts to devour them.

CHAPTER TWENTY-EIGHT:

JUDGMENT ON GOG

el reiterated, "In Ezekiel 39: 18 – 23 we can read what happens to Gog just prior to Judgement Day. I know it's a lot of scripture however its vital to read."

Ezekiel 39

18 *"And it will come to pass at the **same time,** when <u>Gog comes against the land of Israel,</u>" says the Lord God, "that My fury will show in My face.*

19 For in My jealousy and in the fire of My wrath I have spoken: 'Surely in that day there shall be
<u>*a great earthquake in the land of Israel,*</u>

20 so that the fish of the sea, the birds of the heavens, the beasts of the field, all creeping things that creep on the earth, and all men who are on the face of the earth shall shake at My presence.

<u>*The mountains shall be thrown down,*</u>
<u>*the steep places shall fall, and*</u>
<u>*every wall shall fall to the ground.'*</u>

*21 <u>I will call for a sword against Gog throughout all **My mountains**,"</u> says the Lord God.*

"Every man's sword will be against his brother.

22 And I will bring him to judgment with <u>pestilence</u> and <u>bloodshed</u>; I will rain down on him, on his troops, and on the many peoples who are with him, <u>flooding rain, great hailstones, fire, and brimstone</u>.

23 Thus I will magnify Myself and sanctify Myself, and I will be known in the eyes of many nations. Then they shall know that I am the Lord.'"

Mel, then recapped saying, "Judgment for Gog and his forces consists of;

1. Pestilence
2. Bloodshed
3. Flooding rain
4. Great Hailstones
5. Fire
6. Brimstone."

Gog and His Magog forces, now all dead.

CHAPTER TWENTY-NINE:

AFTERMATH OF GOG

℣he Israelites from the cities of Israel now plunder and pillage all the wooden items previously mentioned, from the bodies, warehouses, and cities of the dead."

Mel continued, In Ezekiel 39: 9 – 16, the Prophet Ezekiel describes

*9 "Then those who dwell in <u>the cities of Israel</u> will go out and set on fire and burn the weapons, both the shields and bucklers, the bows and arrows, the javelins and spears; **<u>and they will make fires with them for seven years.</u>***

Mel pointed out that at this time there will be cities of Israel not just camps or groups, this indicates their numbers, will be massive.

*10 They will not take wood from the field nor cut down any from the forests, **<u>because they will make fires with the weapons</u>**; and <u>they will</u> **<u>plunder</u>** those who <u>plundered them</u>, and **<u>pillage</u>** those who <u>pillaged them</u>," says the Lord God.*

"Also," Mel said, "as stated above, they will PLUNDER and PILLAGE, from those who in the past plundered and pillaged them.

To put this into perspective, we could generalize as follows,

PLUNDER means to "steal goods from (a person), typically using force in a time of war.

PILLAGE means to rob (a place) using violence, especially in wartime, such as when looters plunder stores."

11 "It will come to pass in that day that I will give Gog a burial place there in Israel, the valley of those who <u>pass by east of the sea</u>; and it will <u>obstruct travelers</u>, because there they will bury Gog and all his multitude. Therefore, they will call it the **<u>Valley of Hamon Gog</u>***.*

12 For **SEVEN MONTHS, the house of Israel will be burying them, in order to cleanse the land.**

13 Indeed <u>all the people</u> of the land will be burying, and they will gain renown for it on the day that I am glorified," says the Lord God.

Mel said; "See we have just read…. **ALL THE PEOPLE…**

14 "They will set apart men regularly employed, with the help of a search party, to pass through the land and bury those bodies remaining on the ground, in order to cleanse it.

<u>At the end of seven months they will make a search.</u>

15 The search party will pass through the land; and when anyone sees a man's bone, he shall set up a marker by it, till the buriers have buried it in the Valley of Hamon Gog.

16 The name of the city will also be Hamonah. Thus they shall cleanse the land."'

Mel added; "See after the majority of bones have been gathered and now buried in the 'Valley of Hamon, Gog search parties will still go out to look for any bones still out there and place a marker on them for the gatherers to collect. This will be the most massive clean-up ever undertaken for no trace of the Anti-God will forever, for ever after and for evermore, exist.

CHAPTER THIRTY:

MAGOG ARMIES DESTROYED

el continued, "Again, this takes place just prior to Judgment Day. "The people's leader is Gog (NORTH) and his forces consisting of his Magog (SOUTH) commanders and soldiers having bows and arrows, plus others of his nations tagging along in hopes of <u>plunder booty</u>."

Now we read about Magog.

Ezekiel 39:6
*And <u>I will send fire on Magog</u> and <u>on those who live in security in the coastlands</u>.
Then they shall know that I am the Lord.*

God will deal with Gog's Magog commanders, his armies and peoples, as they come against Israel. God will also send fire to these peoples of Magog who live in the coastlands, and feel secure. Those living in these coastal regions manufacture the wooden weapons used by Gog and his Magog forces, the following list some of them.

BOWS
ARROWS
SHIELDS
BUCKLERS
JAVELINS
SPEARS

Note. The people living in the cities are burned with fire.

CHAPTER THIRTY-ONE:

JUDGMENT DAY BOOKS OPENED

Mel, using a soft and gentle tone, now said, "This is the last time I will use the phrase, 'cull of the damned'. The evil one, his three beast-demons, his vast armies along with the peoples of the Anti-God, who did not learn from the past, are now part of the past, they exist no more."

Mel continued, "Almost everyone has at some time or another heard the expression Judgment Day or the Judgment Day Books. These books are not good. Those, whose names are recorded in them, will at the appointed time, cease to exist in any form or fashion."

"The Judgment Day Books are now opened, and if your name is still recorded in them you go into oblivion. What a tragic shame for a soul to cease to exist for ever, forever more and forever after, truly an incomprehensible thought, one word may sum it up, 'astonishment'."

CHAPTER THIRTY-TWO:

"BOOK OF LIFE" & "LAMBS BOOK OF LIFE"

"All souls ever created, and who during the 1000-years who, have proven themselves worthy will have had their names <u>erased from the Judgment Day Books</u>, and <u>entered into the Book of Life</u>."

BOOK OF LIFE

"These 'Book of Life souls' now enter a new era, you might say, 'Heaven on Earth' for evil personified has ceased to exist in all forms, and people without exception, are now 'Godly' in all aspects, 'earth is now Godly'," The planet earth will come to be known throughout the cosmos, as 'God's Home'."

"Before I discuss the Book of Life in more detail," Mel added, "the question is, how did a person have their name removed from the Judgement Day Books and into the Book of Life? The answer, their actions were judged during the 1000-Year Kingdom, each one according to their works. Does this mean if they were good people, their names were automatically removed from the Judgement Day Books? No, they were not. Did it mean that bad people were automatically judged and cast into the lake of fire? Not necessarily."

Maria commented, "So all people had the opportunity to repent. I guess an easy matter to comprehend for some, an impossibility for others. I remember the old saying 'birds of a feather flock together' meaning the good gravitated and congregated with good and evil with evil."

Joe added, "So the good were drawn to the light of grace, accepted the offer of salvation and received garments of salvation, evil however as usual, rejected."

Mel said, "All Christians and most other religions of the world have heard about Judgement Day. The following is recorded in the Bible:

Revelation 20: 11-15
Then I saw a great white throne and Him who sat on it, from whose face the earth and the heaven fled away. And there was found no place for them.

And I saw the dead, small and great, standing before God, <u>and books were opened</u>. And <u>another book was opened, which is the Book of Life</u>. And the dead were judged according to their works, by the things which were written in the books.

*The sea gave up the dead who were in it, and
Death and Hades delivered up the dead who were in them.
And they were judged, each one according to his works.*

Then Death and Hades were cast into the lake of fire. This is the second death.

<u>And anyone not found written in the Book of Life was cast into the lake of fire.</u>"

Mel said; "The Judgment Day book(s) contains every human being from Adam to Judgement Day, excluding two other groups that I will soon discuss. This is the official record of all human life, every soul, and that in itself is amazing."

"Now look, every one of the dead, were judged according to their works, by the things which were written in the books. Those having their names in the Judgement Day book, were then, along with Death and Hades, cast into the lake of fire, and for these people this is the second death, oblivion.

You're seeing it live, human spirits devolving into oblivion."

Maria asked, "This is revolting to look at, and why are we seeing it?"

"Now," Mel smiled saying, "There is another most glorious book:

LAMB'S BOOK OF LIFE

"In the Lamb's Book of Life are those who matured from Bride of Christ into the Wife of Christ and now, are the Royal Kings, Royal Priests and Priests of God, truly a Holy Nation redeemed from Earth. Everyone is a Priest of some category and eternally they serve their God and His Son. They have ongoing unique functions.

CHAPTER THIRTY-THREE

ISRAEL RESTORED TO THE LAND

" **J**n Ezekiel 39 in the Bible we read selected pertinent verses what God has to say about the Nation of Israel that lived in the 12 tribes that surrounded the New Jerusalem.

Remember Mel said, "The Nation of Israel will witness the destruction of Gog, and his Magog nations. Now this group are still in their human bodies and will live eternally.

Maria asked, "What happens if the earth becomes congested in the future?

Mel smiled, saying, "It's a large cosmos." Now let's continue reading.

"I will set My glory among the nations; all the nations shall see My judgment which I have executed, and My hand which I have laid on them. 22 So the house of Israel shall know that I am the Lord their God from that day forward.

Continuing, Mel said, "The nations will see and experience Gods Glory as was in the early days of the Garden of Eden, only this time humanity has now come to a fuller understanding of God. There are many further details concerning the future, and the details are best left to a future time."

"Therefore thus says the Lord God: 'Now I will bring back the captives of Jacob, and have mercy on the whole house of Israel; and I will be jealous for My holy name—after they have borne their shame, and all their unfaithfulness in which they were unfaithful to Me, when they

dwelt safely in their own land and no one made them afraid. When I have brought them back from the peoples and gathered them out of their enemies' lands, and I am hallowed in them in the sight of many nations, then they shall know that I am the Lord their God, who sent them into captivity among the nations, but also brought them back to their land, and left none of them captive any longer. And I will not hide My face from them anymore; for I shall have poured out My Spirit on the house of Israel,' says the Lord God."

Mel concluded, "At the appointed time God said, *'And I will not hide My face from them anymore; for I shall have poured out My Spirit on the house of Israel,' says the Lord God.'"*

CHAPTER THIRTY-FOUR:

NEW HEAVEN AND EARTH

Mel continued, "Once again the Garden of Eden in its full glory and splendor, is established worldwide, the word 'death' no longer has any meaning, truly Heaven on Earth. The following Biblical passages relate to a New Heaven and Earth."

The Glorious New Creation

Isaiah 65:17
"For behold, I create new heavens and a new earth; And the former shall not be remembered or come to mind.

Isaiah 66:22
"For as the new heavens and the new earth Which I will make shall remain before Me," says the Lord, "So shall your descendants and your name remain.

2 Peter 3:13
Nevertheless, we, according to His promise, look for new heavens and a new earth in which righteousness dwells.

Revelation 21:1 NKJV All Things Made New

21 Now I saw a new heaven and a new earth, for the first heaven and the first earth had passed away. Also, there was no more sea. 2 Then I, John, saw the holy city, New Jerusalem, coming down out of heaven from God, prepared as a bride adorned for her husband. 3 And I heard a loud voice from heaven saying, "Behold, the tabernacle of God is with men, and He will dwell with them, and they shall be His people. God Himself will be with them and be their God. 4 And God will wipe away every tear from their eyes; there shall be no more death, nor sorrow, nor crying. There shall be no more pain, for the former things have passed away."

Mel added, "Here are two last statements of God."

Then He who sat on the throne said, "Behold, I make all things new." And He said to me, "Write, for these words are true and faithful."

And He said to me
"It is done! I am the Alpha and the Omega,
the Beginning and the End...

CHAPTER THIRTY-FIVE:

THE GARDENS OF GOD

Mel's voice was heard saying, "Now, it's your time, look over there, what do you see?"

Maria answered saying, "I see our Heavenly Father, His Son, His Wife and the Holy Spirit which by the way has your exact eyes. I always had the feeling you were more than you appeared, and now I understand who you really are."

"Well done. Now, I have much to show you, look to the Heavens, what you see are the Gardens of Light."

Our Lord said to His Wife; "Come join my Father and........, now, I didn't see that one coming they all thought" The countenance of the three now beamed with absolute radiance, such a brilliance that human eyes would not be able to look directly at them. They were speechless.

Immediately Maria, Joe and Tom were surrounded by many millions or billions, yet one. Now the "Wife" heard the words creation pined for, since Adam; "*Well done, good and faithful servant; you were faithful over a few things, I will make you ruler over many things. Enter into the joy of your lord.*"

Following are the last two verses of the last book of the Bible,

"I Am Coming Quickly,
He who testifies to these things says, "Surely I am coming quickly."
Amen. Even so, come, Lord Jesus!
The grace of our Lord Jesus Christ be with you all. Amen.

"This is the end of the Bible, and this book."

Chapter Thirty-Six:

EPILOGUE

The Holy Trinity and God's Children gazed outwards; the cosmos, bowed.

Joe softly meckered, "Never did get my book deal." Once again Joe experienced a spiritual rib-jab from someone "Hey I felt that".

Maria sighed, "I'll keep him on a short leash." Someone else chuckled softly, "You wanted him, you got him. Tomorrow we'll discuss your book deal."

Joe, nudged Maria "Did you hear that? See there still may be a book deal."

Maria whispered to Joe, "Yes tomorrow we'll talk about it further." Joe beamed with delight until Maria whispered in his ear, "Remember Joe, forever, forevermore and forever after, is only day one, of eternity. "

Joe countered, filled with excitement, and said, "I get it now, I now know how to actually recall the day that has passed".

Maria looked at Tom then back at Joe. "Oh no! Where's Joe?" she said. "I don't know," replied Tom, "but here comes.........!"

Maria gasped, "What did Joe just say to you?"

Tom sighed, "Something like, Geronimo!"

"Never should have elaborated on time travel with him.", Mel meckered.

Seems like Joe got in the last word, as usual.

"Just great." Maria meckered, "Let's get pen and paper. It seems we're going to need it."

Tom chuckled; "Prequel?"

Someone else commented in a muted but exasperated tone, "You couldn't leave well enough alone, you just had to mention 'book deal', really!"

"I need a Scotch!"

Tom looked at Maria, who then looked at Mel and they all laughed. They didn't say it, but did they think it?

The cosmos roared, "Here we go again!"

CHAPTER THIRTY-SEVEN:

"THE EXODUS PROTOCOL"

pearheaded by 'Geronimo Joe', pen, and paper or rather...
his eyes.

"THE EXODUS PROTOCOL"

Presidential Executive Order DT666

SYNOPSIS

Tom, during the gathering of data for his soon to be published book series entitled "The Rapture Chronicles", researched what the Presidential Executive Order DT666 meant and was shocked to discover that its roots originated from, Latin. Something like 'Draconis Assignare' that to the best of my knowledge means "The Dragons Seal or Mark. In the book, this is referred to as the "Dragon's Tattoo 666". This is the three-color evil-logo of the sea-beast aka Satan's son, the false prophet and those who take his mark in pride or fear.

Tom unwittingly contacted sources who were secretly the anti-Christ strategically placed within the world, and only to be activated in part due to potential threatening testimony by Christians. This triggers many assassination attempts that eventually come to his awareness, causing him to become paranoid. Tom is not alone as many other scientists proclaiming contrary ideas were also targeted and marked for death, by these anti-God assassins.

Each time Tom makes a furtive discovery, they come with a price. As the anti-God, agencies now focus their attention on him and anyone else helping him, their agenda is to intimidate, harass, discredit, and if that does not work, kill.

Maria and Joe are dragged into Tom's nightmare, as peculiar events begin surrounding and impacting upon their safety. Joe for some reason has trouble sleeping. He is viewing many strange dream-state events that continuously cause him to bolt awake. Soon his dream-state visions begin during his waking hours and scares the hell out of him. Seemingly, supernatural forces are trying to either kill or protect them, and at times, it is difficult to distinguish which is which.

Notwithstanding these events, Maria and Joe, still think Tom's a little nuts, however they cannot explain Joe's visions.

Maria, begins to record all of Joe's visions into a daily diary, that unbeknownst to both of them will be the content and foundation, of Joe's future book,

"THE EXODUS PROTOCOL"
if it ever gets published.

Soon a library incident takes place whereby all doubts are removed, as far as Tom is concerned. As the weeks turn into months, we see the anti-God throughout the USA and around the world systematically begin targeting firstly the Christians, then anyone challenging their agenda. The anti-God view Christians as terrorists and begin placing their names into confidential files that in time are intended to become public. It seems that while the constitution of the USA says,

"In God We Trust"
The question now is… "In What God Do You Trust?"

The more devout Christians are, the more they are painted as possible terrorists, and soon travel is restricted to them. The State implements guidelines for the many thousands of religious organizations in an attempt to root out possible cult-terrorists, hiding in plain sight. At first the State takes over how religious sermons will be conducted including their contents. The established religions must have their hierarchy certified by the State-run agency every three months, failing which, they are decertified. Should any decertified preacher then be caught, they are quickly arrested as anti-government agents, and most just disappear.

The "emergency disaster shelters" known as "FEMA" are strategically located within the United States and Canada along with its sister hellhole in Alaska. These so-called 'emergency shelters' now take on a sinister role. They quickly become detention and interrogation camps for Christians. All prior terrorists have been recruited by secret government agencies and let loose to do the bidding of these agencies. They only report to one, the President. He will soon be known as

The...
False President, Satan's son Leo... the world will call him "The Beast".

The closer to Pentecost Sunday, the seemingly impossible begins to take place, as once clandestine agencies along with their evil agendas become visible. The anti-God declares themselves as the good, and everyone else the bad, (or as Tom is quoted as saying; "Evil Masquerading as Good").

Events rapidly ramp up to the title of this book, with "The Exodus Protocol" with its Executive Order DT666. Now, the axis of evil takes root and sprouts, a precursor to atrocities to come. Any attempt to describe these events in a few lines of text would be inadequate, to say the least.

One last note, the then current President of the United States of America is not who you think, call it happenstance or whatever you like. The circumstances surrounding his catapult to global totalitarian power is best described as diabolical, how this could ever happen, remember the old axiom...

"Be careful what you Wish for."

The population, is being deceived by evil (we read in the Bible that in the end time God will send them strong delusion, and they will believe the lies) and for the most part it is "business as usual."

THE END

Availability of this book is subject to intervention by a Very High Power, until the Rapture after-which it will be banned under penalty of death, by the Unholy Trinity, Amen.

ENDNOTES

1. Revelation 19:9-10 THE MARRIAGE SUPPER

Then he said to me, "Write: 'Blessed are those who are called to the marriage supper of the Lamb!'" And he said to me, "These are the true sayings of God." 10 And I fell at his feet to worship him. But he said to me, "See that you do not do that! I am your fellow servant, and of your brethren who have the testimony of Jesus. Worship God! For the testimony of Jesus is the spirit of prophecy."

2. Revelation 19:6-8 THE LORD'S WIFE

And I heard, as it were, the voice of a great multitude, as the sound of many waters and as the sound of mighty thunderings, saying, "Alleluia! For the[d] Lord God Omnipotent reigns! 7 Let us be glad and rejoice and give Him glory, for the marriage of the Lamb has come, and His wife has made herself ready." 8 And to her it was granted to be arrayed in fine linen, clean and bright, for the fine linen is the righteous acts of the saints.

3. God makes all things new.

Revelation 21: 1-27

1 Now I saw a new heaven and a new earth, for the first heaven and the first earth had passed away. Also there was no more sea. 2 Then I, John, saw the holy city, New Jerusalem, coming down out of heaven from God, prepared as a bride adorned for her husband. 3 And I heard a loud voice from heaven saying, "Behold, the tabernacle of God is with men, and He will dwell with them, and they shall

be His people. God Himself will be with them and be their God. 4 And God will wipe away every tear from their eyes; there shall be no more death, nor sorrow, nor crying. There shall be no more pain, for the former things have passed away."

5 Then He who sat on the throne said, "Behold, I make all things new." And He said to me, "Write, for these words are true and faithful." 6 And He said to me, "It is done! I am the Alpha and the Omega, the Beginning and the End. I will give of the fountain of the water of life freely to him who thirsts. 7 He who overcomes shall inherit all things, and I will be his God and he shall be My son. 8 But the cowardly, unbelieving, abominable, murderers, sexually immoral, sorcerers, idolaters, and all liars shall have their part in the lake which burns with fire and brimstone, which is the second death."

9 Then one of the seven angels who had the seven bowls filled with the seven last plagues came to me and talked with me, saying, "Come, I will show you the bride, the Lamb's wife." 10 And he carried me away in Spirit to a great and high mountain, and showed me the great city, the holy Jerusalem, descending out of heaven from God, 11 having the glory of God. Her light was like a most precious stone, like a jasper stone, clear as crystal. 12 Also she had a great and high wall with twelve gates, and twelve angels at the gates, and names written on them, which are the names of the twelve tribes of the children of Israel: 13 three gates on the east, three gates on the north, three gates on the south, and three gates on the west. 14 Now the wall of the city had twelve foundations, and on them were the names of the twelve apostles of the Lamb. 15 And he who talked with me had a gold reed to measure the city, its gates, and its wall. 16 The city is laid out as a square; its length is as great as its breadth. And he measured the city with the reed: twelve thousand furlongs. (my calculation = 1500 miles) Its length, breadth, and height are equal. 17 Then he measured its wall: one hundred and forty-four cubits, according to the measure of a man, that is, of an angel. 18 The construction of its wall was of jasper; and the city was pure gold, like clear glass. 19 The foundations of the wall of the city were adorned with all kinds of precious stones: the first foun-

dation was jasper, the second sapphire, the third chalcedony, the fourth emerald, 20 the fifth sardonyx, the sixth sardius, the seventh chrysolite, the eighth beryl, the ninth topaz, the tenth chrysoprase, the eleventh jacinth, and the twelfth amethyst. 21 The twelve gates were twelve pearls: each individual gate was of one pearl. And the street of the city was pure gold, like transparent glass.

The Glory of the New Jerusalem

22 But I saw no temple in it, for the Lord God Almighty and the Lamb are its temple. 23 The city had no need of the sun or of the moon to shine in it, for the glory of God illuminated it. The Lamb is its light. 24 And the nations of those who are saved shall walk in its light, and the kings of the earth bring their glory and honor into it. 25 Its gates shall not be shut at all by day (there shall be no night there). 26 And they shall bring the glory and the honor of the nations into it. 27 But there shall by no means enter it anything that defiles, or causes an abomination or a lie, but only those who are written in the Lamb's Book of Life.

4. THE MOUNT OF TRANSFIGURATION "GOD SPEAKS"
"This is My Beloved Son in whom I am well pleased 'hear him'"

These magnificent words resound as thunderous-lightning throughout Eternity. They were spoken about one-year prior the crucifixion of God's Son.

What do these words '**hear him**' signify that were spoken upon the Mount of Transfiguration and who heard them?

As to who were present

FROM TIME

Apostles

Peter

James

John

FROM ETERNITY

Moses

the great teacher of the law

Elijah

the great defender of the law

At this time Moses and Elijah are instructed by God to Hear His Son. The theme of salvation has been consistent starting with John the Baptist, then Jesus, then His disciples and now with His Apostles.

"Repent, for the kingdom of heaven is at hand."

Moses and Elijah were brought by God from eternity to the Mount of Transfiguration who then visibly saw Jesus and heard God speaking, "This is My Beloved Son in whom I am well pleased 'hear him'". Now when these Two Witnesses return to eternity, they testify to all that they were in the presence of God, and God commanded all to now Hear His Son.

At this time Moses and Elijah, God's Two Witnesses, saw and heard, God speaking to His Son.

"This is My Beloved Son in whom I am well pleased 'HEAR HIM'"

Now, these Israelite souls in eternity are taught about God's Plan of Salvation and are told that during a time soon to come, the 1000-Year Kingdom, that God will bring them back to life and that they will have a second opportunity to prove their love and loyalty to Him.

"As to the question 'did all in eternity accept the testimony offered by Moses and Elijah? The answer is no!"

Mel concluded saying, the foregoing supplies some information as to where the different categories of souls came from, who exist during the 1000 years.

**I am MelChizedek,
forever, forever more and forever after.
Pray we meet in Heaven not earth.**